The Picture Frame
and Other Stories

Also by Robert Drake

Fiction

Amazing Grace (1965; 1980; 25th anniversary edition, 1990)
The Single Heart (1971)
The Burning Bush (1975)
Survivors and Others (1987)
My Sweetheart's House: Memories, Fictions (1993)
What Will You Do for an Encore? and Other Stories (1996)

Memoir

The Home Place: A Memory and a Celebration
(1980; the restored text, 1998)

Criticism

Flannery O'Connor: A Critical Essay,
Contemporary Writers in Christian Perspective (1966)

The Picture Frame and Other Stories

Robert Drake

* * *

MERCER UNIVERSITY PRESS
2000

ISBN 0-86554-689-4   MUP/H510

The paper used in this publication meets the minimum
requirements of American National Standard for Information Sciences—
Permanence of Paper for Printed Library Materials, ANSI Z39.48-1984.

Library of Congress Cataloging-in-Publication Data

The picture frame and other stories / by Robert Drake.

Isbn 0-86554-689-4

Contents

(Titles followed by the name of a book or periodical
have already appeared or will duly appear in those sources.)

The Picture Frame

One thing you notice again and again, though, in the old family photographs: how many people are crowded into them. To be sure, Uncle John liked to photograph individuals . . . but he liked nothing so much as a "group" picture, especially a family group—and no family more than the Drakes. It was as though there he could squeeze them all together into one picture frame, into some sort of little world, could put them all together so they would never, for the moment, be parted, never know the pangs of separation which must and would come in time—as though he were striking some sort of private bargain with God. ("Just let me get them all together one more time, all under one roof, for the record, and then You may do as You please!") And there they would be, teeming with life and vitality and about to explode from the picture frame. . . .

[In] the group pictures, we are all there—as though Uncle John had literally gone out into the highways and byways and compelled us to come in—for the *record*. Sometimes, there would even be a stray neighbor or two: Uncle John—and all the Drakes, for that matter—were great *includers* rather than *excluders*. They wanted as many folks in the group as possible—family or not. . . . Loving one another so deeply, secure in the affection so freely bestowed, never feeling that the well might—or could—run dry, they wanted to bring the whole wide world into their circle, into the photographs if it could be done. And really, I think, they almost did.

—from "The Picture Frame," *The Home Place*

* * *

This book is dedicated to the memory of
Signa Crihfield Hardy
and her colleagues at Ripley High School
who showed us the way.

All This Material—A Foreword

"Now why don't you take all this material and just turn it into a novel?" asked my old friend, one of the most distinguished of twentieth-century American literary critics, as he looked over a batch of what blue-haired dowagers have often called my "little stories." And all I could think of for a moment was my mother's going up to the second floor of Goldsmith's department store in Memphis every spring to consult her old friend, Miss Mag Boling, who worked in piece goods, about what sort of "material" she ought to buy for the coming summer's "nicest" dress—what she could wear to both church and the Tuesday Bridge Club. Then after she had made her purchase, even with Miss Mag's advice and counsel a difficult decision, she would take it back home to Woodville, to have her dressmaker, Miss Susie Lankford, make it up—and usually according to a *Vogue* pattern, because, she said, they were considered the best: they never went out of style.

Well, the analogy may not be perfect, but that's the way I always felt about my friend's query. Because I didn't think the "material" and the pattern, the form and the substance of my stories were two different things but somehow complements, which constituted a unified whole. (Hadn't Aristotle said something to that effect?) Anyway, it was what, in teaching my students in literary criticism, I referred to as the heresy of the *beautiful envelope*, the belief that form was just a beautiful envelope to encase the substance and the theme as such was a somewhat immaterial consideration as far as the arts went. And I've never understood why my friend took the line he did in this instance: nobody I've ever known had more respect for what Conrad called the "perfect blending of form and substance" than he did. And from anybody else such a question would have seemed the depth of ignorance, and I've puzzled about it for a good many years now.

In any case, I wonder whether it doesn't conceal some sort of prejudice on his part—in his case, a speculation extremely hard to entertain—against the short story as a form and perhaps an unstated conviction that it's only the start toward a novel the author can't finish, some sort of literary abortion, because of defective ambition or even, God help me, timidity or sloth. Americans, especially, like big things—big and bold, I may say. And I've seen—and heard— critics go into agonies of contortion, trying to come to some real hard and fast distinction between the two forms—the story and the novel—which will settle matters once and for all. But always I myself go back to what I once heard Robert Penn Warren say in differentiating between the two: a short story, he said, is simply a story that's shorter than some other one and, though he didn't add it, perhaps amounts mainly to a difference in length but not necessarily in depth. That's all the distinction I need. But there remains, for many readers, some sort of implicit judgment that, in the arts, anything that's short can't be very serious and you'll just have to learn to live with such a misapprehension.

Well, I decline to take that option as my only choice, and I'll come out loud and bold and say, for all the world to hear—if it really cares—that I write short stories not because I can't write novels (though in dealing with some impertinent inquisitors I often say it's because I have a short attention span) but because I don't want to: they are not the right form for the narratives, the "material" I have to tell. (Can you imagine Chekhov trying to turn "The Darling" or "The Kiss" into any other form or Saki writing anything much but the "short, short" masterpieces starring Reginald or Clovis which are almost anecdotal in their form? But look where they first appeared— in newspapers, both authors. And nobody seems to have thought less of them for doing so.) But can you imagine such a venue today for writers of such distinction? Perhaps *The New Yorker*, itself a kind of newspaper—and one not always without spot or wrinkle, might serve as an analogy here. But I wouldn't want to push it too far. So are we left with the chicken-versus-egg dilemma or shall we just say who cares which of the two considerations—theme or form—comes first; they just have to go together and that's that? And to require anything else of them would be plain stupid—and just as idiotic as trying to dispense with first-person narration for some other point of view in, say, *Huckleberry Finn* or, yea, verily, even *Moby Dick*. *Theme* and *form* are equally important. And there's an end on it, as far as I am concerned.

But back now to my own case—my own "little stories." To start, I should say what many people already know—that I never dreamed of writing such things. I was trained to be a scholar and critic, a teacher, a professor in a university. But about the time I started out in the profession I began—at the suggestion of an older colleague—to try my hand at writing fiction. But look what it was, the sort it was and the attitude it embodied and, above all, the world it came out of, which was all Southern and nearly altogether oral. As long as I could remember, I had been listening to my father and his four brothers, especially, telling tales from the family past, their own and their father's too. (And since their father was a Confederate veteran who had been at Appomattox, one didn't have to be urged to hear anything he had to tell.) Some of these family stories were funny, the rest not necessarily so, indeed often grim or even grotesque. And I know now they grew out of the same atmosphere, the same climate as Sut Lovingood's or, for that matter, Mark Twain's. Not that they were conscious of any such *influences* or any other *literary* considerations. It simply—their style, their attitude—came inevitably out of their way of life, their way of looking at the world. And it would never have occurred to them that it was consciously chosen because of any ulterior considerations. It was a larger-than-life world they saw and told about, sometimes a violent and dangerous one and, for that matter, not so far removed, whether in time or in place, from the frontier. A great deal of it, I think, was based on laughing to keep from crying. And behind it all—the rock, the foundation of both the humor and the conviction—was the human voice, always talking, whether on front porches in hot summer nights or in the smoking cars then reserved for "gentlemen" on the trains of the day and always of course the barrooms in every hamlet or town where liquor was "legal"—and also where it was not.

And more and more I'm convinced that underneath it all lay a firm, but not necessarily articulated, belief in the doctrine of Original Sin as embodied in their professed belief in orthodox Christianity. And I don't believe they would have had any trouble agreeing with Willie Stark's bold assertion that man is conceived in sin and born in corruption and he passeth from the stink of the didie to the stench of the shroud. And I think, by and large, this is what differentiates Southern from Northern humor to this day. Remember that I took my doctorate at Yale and began my teaching career first at the University of Michigan, then at Northwestern. I can't speak for the present time, but in my day I felt pretty much a member of the American Resistance Movement at all three institutions, where despite their great distinction in the arts and sciences, there still seemed to be a vast number of people, both faculty and students, who devoutly believed that if you just had enough "facilities"—libraries, laboratories, and of course always *money*—you would probably in due course be able to raise the dead. And of course remember that, unlike Southerners, they had never been on the losing side of anything: they had never heard the word "no."

I've often wondered in recent years what changes the Viet Nam War brought to those campuses. I gather from brief visits back there that it was not without some enlightening consequences: historian C. Vann Woodward has suggested as much. But I do know that the two regions still laugh at different things, still perhaps are shocked by different things, the North still more easily shocked than the South. But then what else can you expect from people who still, many of them, believe in the perfectibility of man?

But back now to the Southern "voice," the voices of my narrators. The concept of voice of course implies a *performer*, and there were many such in that world, my uncles' and my own—folks who knew how to tell a good tale, who weren't above spicing it up, making it more dramatic, and of course funnier—or sadder—than it began. And they all of them knew what constituted a good tale, indeed who were the best tale-tellers in their own communities. All such knowledge, such criteria went unstated of course—probably not even capable, at least for them, of being put into words. But they knew it when they heard it. And they learned from each other—from the community itself, by means of what some critics have called *the communal discipline of taste*. And one wonders whether such a possibility even exists today, within a culture so diverse as ours and so devoid of common assumptions about man and his world.

If it does, it's often found in the town, the village, one which some would consider "backward" or even illiterate, certainly in no way sophisticated or cosmopolitan. *Community* is a word they hardly seem to understand; yet it never seems to occur to them that nothing in the world of entertainment today is predicated on the concept of community more than the movies of Woody Allen—and a very limited one it is too. (I must confess that I do enjoy them but usually against my will!) And I recall that Joan Baez once observed that there was no such thing as a Republican folk song, which reveals an ignorance of what the very idea of "the folk" is all about.

Yet good things still come out of Nazareth; and you don't have to have "been there, done that," in the parlance of these times, to speak—or write—with authority. (Think of Stephen Crane or Jane Austen, for that matter.) What you do need, what you must have is a good sense of drama, as I once reminded a very famous football coach when he said that, though he wasn't at that time an Episcopalian, he enjoyed going with his wife to their services because of all their "parading around" and such like. And I told him he obviously liked *drama* and ought to remember that he himself was presiding over one of the biggest of all dramas every Saturday during the fall. But that's where it all begins—with real life and three-dimensional human beings, who are *frum* somewhere, as Flannery O'Connor once stipulated, at a certain time, a certain place; and also of course with every writer's inevitable subject—what William

Faulkner called the human heart in conflict with itself. (Why do sports reporters—Ring Lardner, for one—often turn into first-class writers of fiction? Well, for one thing, they're born and bred to have a sharp eye for conflict.)

Well, that's the world I come out of, the background against which I write. And as I've said elsewhere, nothing much *happens* in my stories; and indeed they *are* short—sometimes no more than two or three thousand words. But a completed action, which is the essence of fiction, doesn't depend on length but whether there is meaningful change between beginning and end. And that's all you need.

Surely, because of the oral nature of what interests me, even obsesses me in what I have to tell, my stories are almost bound to be fairly short, indeed couldn't really be otherwise; and I make no apology for that. And I'm especially on guard against all those who don't read them carefully enough to see that, as with Huck Finn, there is often more than one narrative there—one, the surface one, the narrator knows he's telling and another, what you might call the subterranean one, he often doesn't realize he's telling (sometimes not altogether complimentary to himself either). But the story as such is neither one nor the other but both, in a sort of counterpoint, where they complement each other in a seamless combination which constitutes the whole. (Remember that Agatha Christie's Hercule Poirot says that if you just let a murderer talk long enough, no matter what the subject, he will sooner or later give himself away. And Jesus himself says, "Out of thine own mouth will I judge thee.")

I think you'll find that most tale-tellers and tale-writers of the kind I've suggested here are themselves great—and gifted—listeners too. That's how they perfect and refine their own art; they don't necessarily hog the floor. And like all artists, of whatever persuasion, they take from what they hear what may be suitable for their own tales. The word, *tale*, by the way, is one which comes naturally to me in talking about my work, not necessarily in the sense of country stores and cracker barrels—what one of my friends has referred to as the "*aw shucks* school." But it does suggest to me the oral and perhaps intimate nature of its existence and something of the limited things it attempts. But as in folk tales and ballads, those very limitations can suggest or imply a very great deal—often literally matters of life and love and death. And to those who object that they often can't *see* the characters I write about, I say, well, just listen to them *talk* and then you'll know how they look!

Sometimes also they observe that I often don't take Henry James's advice about *showing*, not *telling* in what you write, indeed that I quite often use indirect discourse more than "the real thing." And to them I reply that the sort of thing I do is what it is and doesn't necessarily have to be shown. It operates on different assumptions from James's fiction; and it's perfectly capable of being seen through my particular point of view which is often that of the first-person narrator, who speaks at some remove from the immediate action and not always with what may seem scrupulous attention to chronolgy or even unity of plot—and who often by seemingly irrelevant digressions in anecdotes and asides tells us more than he knows not only about the participants in the story but also about himself and the whole community—hearsay testimony, you might say, which one discounts at his peril because the scope of the narrative may be much wider than he has assumed.

Look briefly at what that mistress of the technique, Eudora Welty, can do here. In "Why I Live at the P.O.," "Sister," the postmistress-narrator, in dramatizing "Mama's" adamant defense of the younger sister, Stella-Rondo's, leaving her husband, "Mr. Whitaker," and arriving back in China Grove, Mississippi, with an "adopted" child whose existence she has never revealed to the family, says

> "Just like Cousin Annie Flo. Went to her grave denying the facts of life," I remind Mama.
>
> "I told you if you ever mentioned Annie Flo's name I'd slap your face," says Mama, and slaps my face.
>
> "All right, you wait and see," I says.
>
> "I," says Mama, "*I* prefer to take my children's word for anything when it's humanly possible."

You ought to see Mama, she weighs two hundred pounds and has real tiny feet. [Italics added.]

And again, in *The Ponder Heart*, Edna Earle, the narrator, discovers Uncle Daniel, the sweet but none-too-bright relative for whom she is part-niece and part-keeper, "loose" on the midway at the Fair, after belting her into the Ferris Wheel,

> up on the platform of the Escapades side-show, right in the middle of those ostrich plumes. . . . passing down the line of those girls doing their come-on dance out front, and handing them out ice cream cones, right while they were shaking their heels to the music, not in very good time. *He'd got the cream from the Baptist ladies' tent—banana, and melting fast.* [Italics added.]

Thus our "seeing" is often filtered through the ear as much as the eye; and the comic, "irrelevant" asides jolt us back into the real, down-to-earth world which, in our momentary departure from sense, we run the risk of leaving behind. Again, Shakespeare says it best: "by indirections find directions out." Different strokes for different folks indeed.

Finally, it's not how much you write—how topical, how timely, sensational or otherwise—that gives us distinguished fiction; rather, it's how valid your story is—how true, an option, says Conrad, about which you may have forgotten to ask. And it requires no less skill, no less talent, even genius than the "big one," as some cut-rate critics refer to the novel. All right, so the world seems to value the longer work: it's more ambitious and often more celebrated in our culture. And yes, we'd all like to have a big, fat best-seller and make lots of money. Who wouldn't? Surely, we all want to live well, and perhaps the house needs a new roof and the baby needs new shoes. But should that be our first object here? I think, finally, we must write what we must and as we must, in the form that it alone compels us to. Anything else involves misrepresentation, even falsification. And neither art nor truth will have anything to do with that.

Alone

At sixty Jim Burk's life was turning out just like he had expected years ago. In the first place, he was born in his parents' middle age (his father was forty-five and his mother was forty) and he was an only child. And so he knew right from the start that in all probability he would lose his parents well before his contemporaries lost theirs. And of course this was the most frightening thing he could think of: the loss of a parent is surely the worst fear that can plague any child. And he wondered—sometimes dreamed—about what would happen if they died before he was grown—how he would manage, where he would live, all the things that centered on his being *alone* from then on out.

He wasn't sure just how he came by this conclusion, but since his earliest memory he had gotten used to thinking of himself as being a loner. And indeed he couldn't easily imagine any other kind of life for himself in later years. But he wasn't unhappy; rather, somehow he was fairly comfortable. He knew how to deal with older people, what they liked, what they feared. Because after the years of his childhood he was thoroughly used to his mother and father and what they said and what they thought about most things. And he knew he was picking up some of their attitudes before he had even had time to examine them in and for himself. So there were just the three of them, facing the world together. And he didn't worry about what he was *missing* in having few friends his own age to associate with.

Strangely enough, he rarely got lonesome. For one thing, his views on many subjects were different from that of his friends—the views of older persons, he realized. And in many ways they made more sense than what his own friends thought. No one ever had to tell Jim about Santa Claus: he seemed never really to have believed in him from the beginning. For that matter, it seemed as though his

life was full of things he either didn't believe in or questioned quite
seriously. Did he really believe in God, did he really believe there
would be a Heaven, and what would it be like anyhow?

O.K., so you got there somehow, by hook or crook; but then
what would you do? One of the biggest questions—maybe even
fears—he had ever had to wrestle with was summed up—and had
been as long as he could remember—in the question "What will you
do for an encore?" How would you keep from getting bored in
Heaven: after you got there—assuming you were lucky enough to do
so—what next? After all, how could you top something as final and
finished as perfection and everlasting bliss? How would you continue
to live, to grow, to expand after you had arrived? And life was
certainly *growth*: he had never had any doubts about that. What
would you do after you took a seat up there? Would you just have to
sit there and listen to God and the archangels preach all day? Would
you lift up your voice in sacred song in the interim? To tell the truth,
what was there to keep you from being bored out of your mind?
Somehow it all reminded him of the old preacher who warned his
congregation to be careful what they prayed for because they were
liable to get it! As Jim grew into the teen years, then the college
ones, he continued to wonder, but with no answers. Was that what
faith was, by the way? Just taking it all like a dose of medicine (like
his mother or Dr. Joe told him to) but wondering whether it would
do him any good after all?

And really where was he to get help back then? His parents were
conventionally Christian people but by no means approaching anything that might be construed as fanatical. And anyway, they didn't
seem to worry about what the good life was: as someone observed,
they and others like them simply *lived* it. And maybe that was the
best thing after all: for all that you might consult the Bible every
hour and every day, *nobody* really *knew* what it might turn out to be.

And Jim was convinced of that opinion when, just before his
baptism at age seven, an old woman down the street scared him half
to death when she told him the way Methodists baptized (by

sprinkling) wasn't really valid: you had to be *immersed*, as was the custom in her own denomination. So what could you do—when doctors disagreed? He didn't really believe that Billy Graham or the pope himself could answer that question. So then you were left right back with yourself, alone.

And for what it was worth, Jim didn't see any way out of his dilemma, whether it was about God or anything else: *nobody* could really tell you what to do. And no, by then he was pretty well assured that he would never find anybody (woman or just plain friend) to "share his life with." And was that just because he didn't trust anybody but himself? Was that the way it was supposed to be? Well, he couldn't answer for *that*, but he never seemed to find an answer to any of these questions. But when he heard people go on about how prayers were answered, whether at church or elsewhere, he always felt like standing up in the middle of the group and saying excuse him, but he was sitting this one out. And like one of his old friends whose own father was a Methodist preacher—and a much beloved one too—he felt like finishing his protest by saying that though he had been praying all his life for guidance, God had never told *him* what to do about anything. Or so it seemed.

And no, he didn't think there would be any Damascus Road revelation for him either. God was just up there, somewhere or other, but did He really *care* about what you did, give you a sign of some sort? Maybe it was all just like that poem of Thomas Hardy's where the speaker protested he would feel a whole lot better if he thought there really was some sort of personage up there whether to bless or to burn (and it didn't really seem to make much difference) instead of what seemed to be just calm and quiet indifference.

So that was more or less the way it all went on for some years until Jim decided that since he couldn't *know* about any of it, he would just have to trust himself and hope for the best. And yes, that would be lonesome too, but what were the options? Without employment, without staying busy there was certainly no help for it anywhere; he knew that much. And yes, God had said it was not good for Man to be alone—perhaps no matter what arrangement he could work out; and Jim had sense enough to see that too. No, you couldn't just live entirely in and for yourself; that way madness would surely lie. (And he had never believed that Henry David Thoreau or Ralph Waldo Emerson or any others of that breed were entirely truthful when they proclaimed their own selfish remedy.) So what was he to do? Well, somehow he had known from way back when that something, he couldn't say what, had always been whispering to him that teaching school might be his resource: you got to work with people, to exchange opinions with them, to even learn from them too—perhaps never to be intimate with them—or for that matter, in his case, anybody else—but in any case at least *connect* with them like some writer (*E. M. Forster*?) had once advised. And perhaps this was true no matter whether you healed the sick or raised the dead, gave sight to the blind or hearing to the deaf. Surely teaching might be something like this and, from his own school days, whether elementary or collegiate, he knew that such messengers had to be special people: to communicate, to reach out and touch someone else, broaden his horizons, and enlighten his darkness—to heal, like Jesus, by *touching*, not *talking*. Surely, this was something of the Good News, whatever the final result. (He already knew you couldn't heal without the cooperation of the patient, who always had the last word.) Yes, he would give it a try.

So he did and with excellent results. The profession he had chosen almost out of desperation turned out to be pretty much what he had hoped, but you couldn't stay in the classroom, couldn't grade papers, do research in the library all the time. Somehow you did have to *connect* with others or dry up. But how to do it? Was it to be found in warm and lasting friendships, and how did they come anyway? Was there no real substitute for what he knew now he really wanted, really needed—*intimacy* and not necessarily the sexual version thereof. Sometimes he felt almost desperate for it—to communicate completely with someone else, to share all he had with *somebody* without restraint? Could there really be any such thing in the here and now or was that asking too much? Predictably, there might be no answers here from God or anybody else. Did it finally come down to there being no such thing as complete fulfillment here, only what we achieved ourselves, which could be only a partial success? Was that what Heaven was for?

Again, no answer; but for the first time, Jim wondered how anybody could expect there to be. You did the best you could; then Somebody else had to take the leftovers and complete the long, hard journey to perfection and fulfillment—your goal, which finally could not be reached without such help, such grace. Even in the best of circumstances, those who seemed to have it all here were sometimes subject to disappointment, sometimes agonizing ones. The doors that closed behind them never to open again when old friends died, the lives that must be supplanted with new ones after they themselves were gone, but never, never just stopping at one's own discretion—perhaps this was all part of the growth, the wider vision we all sought for. Of course still always alone but now with the consciousness, acquired over many years and much effort, the knowledge that it was in one way or another all true, and not just for the individual but all mankind itself.

The Child Prodigy

Everybody said that Johnny Tucker was a child prodigy. He had been taking piano lessons for only a year and a half; and already he had won "state honors," as his mother always put it. His cousin, Mary Anne, who had "graduated in music," which meant giving a "certificate recital" when she was a high school senior, then going on to study at a conservatory in Chicago, was just getting up her first piano class when Johnny started to school, and she wanted him to take lessons. But Johnny's parents thought he was too young then and gave him no particular encouragement. But Mary Anne, always resourceful, went to her grandfather, who was also Johnny's grandfather, and persuaded him to subsidize Johnny's lessons out of the meager pension he received from the State of Tennessee for being a Confederate veteran. (The size of the pension always irked his son, Johnny's father, because he said it was nothing to what the Union veterans—all those "blue-bellied Yankees"—got; but then Johnny's mother said, well, you couldn't very well expect the U.S. government to remunerate the very people who had tried to destroy it. But Mr. Tucker said that didn't have a thing to do with it.)

Anyhow, Johnny's grandfather started "giving" him his first piano lessons—so they could all find out whether or not he was "serious" about his music; and for a while, Johnny did his practicing next door, at their neighbor Mrs. Henry's, before his parents decided whether or not to buy him piano. But when they saw he really was "serious," they went ahead and did so—bought a good, secondhand piano that had been well cared for by an old friend, all of whose children were grown now and married and living away from home.

And so Johnny's lessons began then in earnest, with his father taking over their expense from his grandfather and with now a real upright piano of his own in their living room. (Johnny still burned for a grand piano and vowed to have one some day—mainly just because they looked like their name—"grand.") But when he started taking music lessons in earnest, his mother sat him down just one time and said, "Now, Johnny, your father and I are glad for you to take piano lessons, but you know you must practice every day, like your Cousin Mary Anne says: that's part of the deal, and I never expect to say anything more about it. But the day you stop practicing, that's the day your father and I stop giving you piano lessons." And Johnny understood, and his mother never had to say any more about it.

But then, as his mother always said, Johnny was so sensible: you could always *reason* with him. Johnny knew that was true, but he also hated it: *reason* seemed somehow so unfair, and you knew you couldn't argue about it—a far cry from being told to do something "because I say so," the way some parents did their children. But *reason* somehow gave parents an unfair advantage, and it was as implacable and unyielding as mathematics, which ironically he had always liked for that very reason: you couldn't argue about it.

So Johnny never had to be "spoken to" about his practicing, and right away he began to make real progress. His cousin, Mary Anne, who of course was a good deal older than he was, seemed pleased with his work and, wisely, never gave him any sort of that old sissified stuff to play—all about "Pixies in the Glen" or "Fairies in the Fountain" or anything like that. Right away she started him off with some of the easiest pieces by Bach and Beethoven and Mozart, even when he had to play them in "simplified" versions for beginners. Johnny hated that, though: it seemed like a form of cheating to him.

But the main thing was that he *was* going on with his music, unlike when somebody stopped "taking" and everybody said what a shame, he (or she) didn't "go on with their music." And right away Johnny felt that he was making great strides, easily learning to read music now and "graduating" from one red-backed John Thompson's beginner's book to another, also even those tiresome old "Technic Tales" by a woman named Louise Robyn. He never did like those: they were like trying to cover up a dose of castor oil with orange juice. He much preferred the Czerny exercises or the little Bach pieces, which were *designed* to teach you technique and no bones about it. All his life he had hated cheats: he didn't even like "pass away" for "die."

At the end of his first year, he got to be in the recital, though he was the first one on the program. (The more difficult your piece, the farther down you were. Always there would be some wispy high-school-senior girl who would bring it all to an end with a Chopin etude or a Liszt transcription, and everybody would applaud wildly and say, "That girl can really make that thing talk!") Johnny's own first recital piece was a Bach minuet—again, none of the sissy stuff for him. In fact, the only bad part about any of it—he *did* love music and he loved to play: there was no question about that—was the music club, which he had to go to once a month, with all Mary Anne's other students. That was where they all had to play the pieces they were working on at the time and had to give reports on current musical events and read articles aloud about the hymn of the month and always take up a collection for the Edgar Stillman Kelly Scholarship Fund, which was sponsored by the National Federation of Music Clubs. And everybody was always on his best behavior, with refreshments served afterwards; and Mary Anne always wanted Johnny to call her "Miss Mary Anne" when they were out in public like that, which Johnny thought was awfully tiresome and silly of her. And he said he wouldn't do it for the world, though she *was* his teacher and fifteen years older than he was. Who did she think she was?

But anyhow, during his second year of taking lessons Mary Anne said she would like to enter him in the "competitive festival," which was held in Memphis in the spring, with all those coming out on top eligible to compete in the finals, to be held a couple of weeks later in Nashville. It wasn't really a contest, she said, but a "festival," where the entrants competed not against each other but *themselves*. Johnny thought all that was pretty silly: how could you compete against *yourself* when the very idea of competition meant that you had to have an opponent, an *enemy* even?

But he didn't say anything about that to either Mary Anne or his mother, just went ahead and learned the required piece for his class (Class A, for seven and eight-year olds)—a little Bach dance piece, and also an optional number, which had to be by an American composer and last no longer than three minutes. (And sure enough, there turned out to be a fierce looking old woman sitting on the front row holding an alarm clock, all crouched ready to spring if you exceeded that limit.) But Mary Anne chose something for him called "By Moonlight," which he thought pretty soupy and not so demanding as Bach, who Mary Anne said was always a challenge, no matter how talented you were. But he rather liked it because it did suggest some sort of dreamy, romantic emotion that he was not averse to, deep down inside, like sometimes at the picture show. And it wasn't really sissy, just romantic. And Mary Anne said that if he got a "superior" or "excellent" rating in Memphis, he would get to go on to the finals in Nashville and that if he won first place there, he would get to play at the annual state convention, which would meet that year in Chattanooga, and maybe even have his picture in the paper.

So on a blustery Saturday in March he and Mary Anne went down to Memphis, and he played his two pieces and got a "superior" rating, just like Mary Anne said he would if he worked hard enough. Then he went on to the finals in Nashville, practicing as hard as he knew how during the two weeks between the two festivals; and sure enough, again just like Mary Anne said, he won first place there and got to play at the annual state convention—the youngest performer on the program. And everybody said what a bright future he had, and his picture was in the Memphis *Commercial Appeal*; and his parents got letters from all their old friends, congratulating them on having such a talented son (who had then taken music only a year and a half), and they all said he was going to be a *child prodigy* and how fortunate his parents were. But when Johnny asked them what a child prodigy was, they said it meant an exceptionally talented and gifted child but he certainly mustn't get a swelled head over it because most of it was just hard work anyway; and they quoted Mark Twain, who had written *Tom Sawyer* and *Huckleberry Finn,* which Johnny loved, about genius being one-tenth inspiration and nine-tenths perspiration. But all Johnny had learned from his experiences so far was that if you just worked hard enough, you were bound to succeed: you shouldn't worry about *talent,* which maybe only God understood. *Effort* was what counted, and it would always pay off. It was like an arithmetic problem, really.

And sure enough, the second year he entered the festival, he repeated his success, this time playing another little Bach piece as his required number (and he was proud he could excel at Bach) and, for his optional selection, another piece by an American composer, as the rules required; and this time it was MacDowell's "To a Wild Rose," another romantic piece and in sharp contrast, of course, to the Bach, who Johnny felt always meant business, again, like mathematics. So once more he got to play at the state convention; and again everybody said he undoubtedly *was* a child prodigy already—it wasn't a question of his "going to be one" any more. And surely he must be planning a career in music, surely he must "go on with it," with all the talent he had. Johnny didn't know about that, and his parents didn't say much. They had always said Johnny could do exactly what he wanted to in life; and though his father did have a prosperous insurance business, they would never think of trying to force him into that: he must make up his own mind about his life and his career.

But all the time Johnny wondered: was he really that talented, was he really a child prodigy, was that all there was to anything—just enough hard work and you were home free? Was it finally that simple? And as for the festival's not being a *contest,* that was all a lot of hooey. Certainly, you were competing against the other entrants: after all, only one of you could play at the state convention, and it was silly to say you had only to compete against yourself. How could that be? It was against all the rules of reason and arithmetic.

So the third year he entered the festival, he wasn't exactly cocky: he just felt that, again, with enough hard work, it was all bound to pay off. And he supposed he would win, but he tried to remember not to have a swelled head about it. Pride went before a fall: he knew that from Sunday School. This time he was in Class B—the next one up the line in age and difficulty from Class A. And the required piece was something called "Menuetto Giocoso" (it looked like he just couldn't get away from minuets) and it was by Haydn (and he wished it was by Bach because you always knew where you were with him—like mathematics). And his optional number, again a pretty sentimental American piece called "Romance in A," which didn't *mean* much of anything, was pretty sounds. And this time the contestants and their teachers were told ahead of time that the judges would not even *see* the students play: they would be seated behind a screen so as not to be unduly influenced by seeing a contestant they already knew. But Johnny wondered about that. He didn't mind it, really; on the other hand, he wouldn't have minded if the judges had known who he was and that he had indeed already won "state honors" twice. Already he had learned that quite often nothing in the world succeeded like success.

But anyhow he and Mary Anne went down to Memphis on another raw, rainy Saturday in March; and again he played his pieces—a little uncertain about the Haydn because he never felt sure about those three-against-twos in the "trio" part. And this time another student of Mary Anne's entered the festival too—Caroline Keaton, who was in the same room as Johnny at school and whom he halfway had a crush on. Caroline's mother went along too—Miss Ellen, so kind and gracious and dignified, Johnny always thought she must be like the Virgin Mary, though he *was* a Methodist; at the very least she must be like some sort of royalty. And it was the first time that Caroline had ever taken part in the festival, so Johnny took some pride in showing her the ropes, like the veteran he was. Johnny's own mother stayed at home: she said she knew Johnny would do his best, and that was all that mattered. Johnny didn't quite agree with that, though; if you did your best, why then you ought to *win*, he thought. But he didn't tell his mother that.

But when the judges' decisions were announced, Johnny had made only "very good," which didn't even qualify him to go to the finals in Nashville. But Caroline Keaton received a "superior" rating—the highest one there was. And Johnny was absolutely stunned. He had done his best, he thought; and he had practiced night and day. And he hadn't even qualified for the finals, to say nothing of winning. He was too proud to cry right there in front of his cousin, and he couldn't think of a worse disgrace than crying in front of Caroline. But when Miss Ellen, Caroline's mother, put her arm around him and said she was indeed proud of him because he had done his best, he burst into tears—at the age of nine too.

He couldn't tell Miss Ellen that when you did your best, you ought to win. (But maybe there were always several who thought they had done their best too; all of a sudden that thought occurred to him and he wasn't quite sure what to make of it.) And he couldn't tell her that all his calculations were now thrown into wild disarray—his calculations about life: that two and two always made four and all the answers came out like the ones in the back of the book, that everything ought to work out like arithmetic. And when Miss Ellen went on to say that after all, he had only been competing against himself and he had certainly done that well, he couldn't very well tell her that he had been competing against her own daughter, Caroline, and everybody else in his class. But he knew very well that he had and anybody but a fool ought to have known it too.

A "competitive festival" *was* a contest, no matter what they called it; and a contest naturally had winners and losers, no matter what you called them. And he felt that he ought to have been a winner, from the way he had worked, the way he had tried, the way he had done his best. It didn't any of it make sense, and he felt that maybe he could never trust either Bach or arithmetic again. Whatever the case, the rules somehow just hadn't worked out. But he figured that wasn't his fault; it was maybe just the way of the world, something that he didn't understand right then. But in any case he wasn't going to act like a baby crying about it. So he thanked Miss

Ellen for her kindness in as dignified a manner as he could and then went into the men's room, where he could wash his face and be by himself for a while and think the whole business over and maybe come to terms with what it was that had just happened to him.

The Election

That summer when there was so much talk about the election Tommy Barnes was twelve and his father's old friend, Mr. Bob Dudley, had decided to run for county judge. Old Mr. Joe Fitzpatrick, who had been judge for almost as long as anyone could remember, had finally decided to retire—or, as Tommy's father said, was *being* retired by his family because they wanted to get him ready for Judgment Day. Tommy didn't know what all Mr. Joe Fitzpatrick had done, either as a man or as a county judge, which warranted his needing a course of spiritual rehabilitation before his appointment with his Maker; but it was no worse than anybody else, he supposed.

Of course Mr. Fitzpatrick hadn't been trained in the law: he and his brother had run a livery stable business there in Woodville for years, and after that kind of business played out with the coming of the automobile, they turned to handling tractors and farm implements. And Tommy's father said Old Man Joe, as he always called him, wasn't a particularly *bad* man; he was just an ordinary mortal who wasn't above turning a blind eye to certain kinds of mischief where people weren't hurting anybody but themselves, or even having his palm crossed with silver under the table to lubricate things every now and then. It wasn't any of it downright *wicked*, Mr. Barnes said, only *weak*, with just a touch of the Old Adam thrown in for good measure. And on the whole, the county hadn't fared too badly under Old Man Joe: they could have done a lot worse. But it was time for him to retire now and make way for the future and the new day that was dawning. And for Mr. Barnes that meant Bob Dudley, who he said was a fine, upstanding Christian gentleman and just what the county needed right then.

Tommy didn't know Mr. Bob very well, but he reckoned his father was right. They were about the same age—in their early forties—and old friends, both of them coming from Maple Grove out in the county; and Mr. Barnes said that anybody that knew how hard Bob Dudley had worked to "make a lawyer," as he put it, would really admire him all the more. He hadn't been able to go off to college or law school but had just regularly come into town—sometimes riding on a mule if no horse was available on his family's place that day—and "read" law in old Captain Conner's office.

Captain Conner was a Confederate veteran who had started practicing law right after the War, when he was barely twenty-one; and in his last years, he had taken a liking to young Bob Dudley, especially because he said young Bob had to make his way in the world, just like he had himself after Reconstruction: no money, no connections, just the brain the good Lord had given him. So he had let Mr. Bob come into his office and read law and even had often given him his old clothes to wear, Mr. Bob had so few of his own. There was no doubt about it, Captain Conner said: Mr. Bob was a deserving young man and he would go far if he just had some boosting in the right place at the right time.

And Mr. Bob did go far. He passed the bar examination with flying colors and then went into partnership with Captain Conner and finally more or less inherited his practice when he passed on. He was very active in all the young people's work at the Methodist Church—the Epworth League—and then the Men's Bible Class after he moved into town and was established in his law practice. Later on, he married Miss Louise Dickinson, who was very pretty and sang in the choir; and they made what everybody called a fine young couple—good looking, both of them, and really *dedicated* to their work and to the community.

From the first, though, Mr. Bob had raised doubts in some people's minds because, they said, he was too much of an *idealist*. Tommy wasn't sure exactly what that was; but when he asked his father, Mr. Barnes said it meant someone who tried to make this tired old world conform to some sort of perfect *ideal* he had off there in space somewhere. And you knew you couldn't ever attain it—not in this world—but it wasn't a bad idea to try, as long as you didn't try too hard or expect too much. But Tommy found that hard to understand: if something *could* be perfect and just like it ought to be, why shouldn't you work to attain it here and now? Wasn't that a good ambition?

But then Mr. Barnes always told Tommy he himself "strived too hard for perfection": all A's on his report card was all very well, but there were other things in life too—like getting out and mixing more with people and learning more about how and why the world turned round. Mr. Barnes didn't seem to think Tommy knew much of anything outside books; and he told him he was riding for a fall some day if he didn't watch out: the world just didn't work that way. Of course Tommy didn't understand because grown people always told you there was nothing more valuable than an education (and Tommy hoped to go to college too). But then, like his father was doing now, they turned right around and told you that it wasn't all in books either.

Tommy did know that sometimes Mr. Bob Dudley got carried away by ideas. Back then, in the thirties, he was always saying that he saw no objection to having Negro clerks in white people's stores and indeed white people had better go on and do a few things like that (where the races were concerned) and do them *now* of their own free will before they *had* to do them later on. But nobody much listened to him then: even Tommy's father said Mr. Bob was too "visionary" at times.

But then one Sunday night, when there was a "union" service for all the churches (always on a fifth Sunday), this time down at the Baptist Church, the Baptist preacher, Dr. Hurt, preached on the text "Absalom, my son" and said it was up to the people of Woodville to take more thought for their children's future, that too many parents today were shirking their duty to their children and sooner or later those same children would prove a *curse* rather than a blessing to them and the time for action was *now*. And Mr. Bob Dudley, who had gotten to be mayor by that time, didn't do a thing after church that night but go out to Summers' Red Star Inn, the local road house on the Memphis highway, and tell Jim Summers that the people of Woodville weren't going to tolerate him and his beer joint any longer, putting temptation in their children's path and leading them astray, and he might as well close up his business right then.

But Jim Summers just laughed in his face and said he reckoned he could weather the storm, and so there was nothing else for Mr. Bob to do but tuck his tail between his legs and come on back to town. (This from Tommy's mother, who had never been all that keen on Mr. Bob: she said he might have his head in the clouds but he'd better learn to keep his feet on the ground.) And even Mr. Barnes conceded that once again Mr. Bob might have been too visionary. But still he was a good man and an old friend, and he would stick by him through thick and thin.

Nobody ever knew what made Mr. Bob decide to run for county judge: by then his law practice kept him busy enough, and he had already been mayor (one term, though, was enough for him, he said). Maybe he just decided the county needed a good sweeping out and cleaning up after Old Man Joe was out of the way. Some people said Mr. Bob had always had political ambitions and they wouldn't be at all surprised if he didn't have his eye on the state legislature in Nashville or even the governor's mansion in due course. But Mr. Barnes said that was all nonsense, Bob Dudley would never overreach himself that much; and, besides, he was too dedicated to Woodville and Barlow County ever to want to leave there. But other people just nodded and smiled like they knew more than anybody else and said they wouldn't be a bit surprised if Bob Dudley got too big for his breeches some day: he had all the earmarks, they said— lots of ambition, a pretty wife, a good law practice and a term as mayor—and he had come all the way from nothing, you might say. Sooner or later, they said, he was going to get his comeuppance.

But Mr. Barnes didn't feel that way; and Tommy certainly hated
to think it might turn out like that because he had always looked up
to Mr. Bob: his father said Mr. Bob's life story would serve as a
lesson for any other young man, to show him what you could do on
your own, without money, without connections—what people called
"pull." So Mr. Barnes more or less went along with Mr. Bob's
campaign for county judge though privately expressing some
reservations about it all to his wife: what did Bob *want* with it
anyway, he said, he ought to be satisfied now. But Mrs. Barnes
would always just say, "Well, you've known him longer than I have.
. . . " And then trail off into silence.

There had been some speculation about whether Mr. Bob would
have any opposition for the race. Some people said, in any case, he
would be a shoo-in; others suggested that what was left of the old
county political machine, though the older ones were dead by now,
wouldn't let Mr. Bob get in if they could possibly help it. While the
old crowd hadn't always had Old Man Joe in their pockets, they
knew they could always count on him—and in many cases, mainly
just to sit there and do nothing, which was one of the things
machines seemed to flourish on. And knowing whom you could
count on was apparently one of the things politics was all about,
Tommy figured. Many people said the machine crowd knew they
couldn't count on Mr. Bob and certainly weren't about to let him get
elected if they could help.

Whatever the case, nobody was prepared for Mr. Bob's opposition to come from the quarter it did—from old Dr. Jennings, who had
been everybody's family doctor in the south end of the county almost
as long as anybody could remember, and a true-blue citizen and an
elder in the Presbyterian Church from the word *go*. He wasn't even
above taking a drink now and then or indulging in a friendly little
card game on the side. But he was certainly a man of his word,
always a man of honor: everybody knew that. Why, everybody in the
county knew about the time, when he was already seventy years old,
that he had knocked out old Mr. Ben Allen's front teeth, for insinu-

ating that he was cheating at cards. ("Ain't nobody in this world going to call me a liar or a cheat!" he had thundered.) And God only knew, Tommy's father said, how many babies Dr. Jennings had delivered, how much doctoring he had done without ever getting a nickel for it: he was just that kind of doctor, that kind of man. But what did *he* want with being county judge? Didn't he have enough to do already—and at his time of life too? And anyway, he wasn't a lawyer: what did he know about the law or anything connected with it? And would he be mostly a rubber stamp for the machine crowd or would he be his own man?

These were the questions that everybody talked about all that hot summer, before the election in August. And Tommy listened intently everywhere he went. He wanted Mr. Bob to win very badly; after all, he was his father's close friend and a model of what an upstanding man ought to be—not so young any more but always ready, he said, to move with the times. He was certainly a man with high ideals, and exactly what you would want in a public figure. And he had done it all on his own too.

On the other hand, Dr. Jennings wasn't a bad man; but he was a man with no legal experience, just lots of medical practice and dealing with folks—more than enough to prevent him from being "visionary" about anything or anybody. Why, there was no more *beloved* man in the county than Dr. Jennings, Mr. Barnes said. Practically everybody owed him something—for free medical care when they couldn't pay (and in those days—the thirties—times were hard enough) or just letting them pay him "in kind" when they could. (Dr. Jennings said he never wanted for country hams in the winter or any kind of fresh produce in the summer.) And Mr. Barnes said, though Dr. Jennings was a Presbyterian elder, there was hardly a man in that end of the county that hadn't had a drink with him at one time or another or maybe even a roll of the dice on occasion. Yes, indeed, he was beloved, which was something, in spite of everything else, you could hardly say about Bob Dudley. But Tommy nevertheless was pulling for Mr. Bob as hard as he could: OK, so he *was* a comparatively young man with high ideals, maybe even "visionary" but one who certainly wanted only what was best for all the people, all the county. And he *was* a lawyer and would know what he was doing. Anything illegal or *unethical* (a word Tommy had picked up from his father) would certainly be beneath him.

So that was one reason Tommy was disturbed when, in the "locals" column of the weekly *Gazette*, where it always told about who was sick or who was visiting whom in town or out, and who had spent the day in Memphis, a few weeks before the election there appeared as a "paid advertisement" the sentence: "You wouldn't send for a lawyer to deliver your baby, so why elect a doctor as your county judge?" And when Tommy asked his father who was responsible for the "ad," Mr. Barnes just said "Mr. Bob's campaign committee." But Tommy knew that was just a group of Mr. Bob's old friends, including his father, and he was worried. Wasn't that the sort of thing people called playing dirty politics? Was that really worthy of Mr. Bob and all he was supposed to stand for?

So Tommy asked his father about it; but Mr. Barnes just replied, "Well, you know, son, they say all's fair in love or war, and that's what politics is—another form of war. And if you get into it, well, you've got to live in the real world, like it really is." But that didn't satisfy Tommy, who felt that Mr. Bob's campaign was somewhat compromised by such doings. He even had some intimations from his friends that their parents felt less than cordial toward Mr. Bob: they said their parents thought he was nothing but an *opportunist* (a word Tommy had to look up in the dictionary) and was finally no better than the old-style "cracker-barrel" politicians and "log rollers" he professed to deplore. And when Tommy asked his father about that, Mr. Barnes just said, "Don't ever forget, son, that Mr. Bob is a *man* just like the rest of us. He's my old and dear friend, and I'd do anything I could for him. Right now I'm doing everything I can to get him elected county judge. But he's not *perfect*, though I think he tries to be harder than he ought. Bob has never really learned to *compromise*, to literally 'play politics'; and that's something each of us has to learn to do, one way or another, every day he lives. And that may be his weakness."

Tommy didn't understand: how could it be a "weakness" to be honest and fair? But he more or less nodded in agreement with his father and then went out and sat on the back porch, where he always went when he had something hard he needed to think over. Everybody in his family was busy with the election now. Mr. Barnes was "working" some of the districts out in the county for Mr. Bob, and Tommy's mother was heading up a group called "Women for Dudley." Tommy wished there was something he could do, but at the age of twelve there was little for him except delivering handbills announcing Mr. Bob's next speech or tacking up Mr. Bob's posters on telephone poles. Once or twice the older people he encountered along the way remonstrated with him for being involved in a political campaign at his age. And all he could say was: "I think Mr. Bob is a good man, and I want to help him in any way I can." But then the grown people would all shake their heads and smile and say: "Sonny, you've got a lot to learn." There were times even when Tommy's mother would lose patience and say she didn't see why anybody in this world would want to go into politics despite its obvious fascination: it was all so dirty, and you knew perfectly well you couldn't touch pitch without being defiled. But Mr. Barnes would just laugh at her then and say that was naive and where had she been all her life?

Nobody would venture to predict the outcome of the election: as the time drew nearer, whatever lead Mr. Bob might have had by announcing early had more or less been eroded by Dr. Jennings' almost universal popularity. But everybody was saying it was too close to call and would go right down to the wire. On the day itself, which was hot and muggy and didn't improve anybody's morale, all the Barnes family were working at the Woodville polls down at the courthouse: handing out Mr. Bob's cards ("Bob Dudley, an experienced lawyer and a proven public servant, solicits your vote and influence") and, in the case of Tommy's father, driving voters without cars to the polls. And Mr. Bob's family were working too: Miss Louise and the two teenage girls were right there at the polls, shaking hands, smiling, and talking to everybody.

At noon everybody took time out for lunch, when the election officers took the ballot boxes over to the Bluebird Cafe across the Square and put them under the tables while they ate. (Tommy thought it was a little like locking up the members of a jury during a trial—like he had heard his father talk about.) And then they were back at it again, all the hot August afternoon, until the polls closed at five.

When the officials began to count the Woodville votes, Mr. Bob was ahead for a while. But then the precincts out in the county began to telephone in their results, and it was apparent long before bed time that Dr. Jennings had won by a substantial margin. Tommy didn't understand it, and he was very much disappointed. Here was an honest, fair-dealing man like Mr. Bob, qualified in every way for the job and an idealist too; and the voters had overwhelmingly rejected him. Didn't they have any sense? What was the matter with them anyway? What was the matter with the world? It was all he could do to keep from crying.

Later, when they had all gotten home from the courthouse, hot and tired after the long day, all he could think of to do right then was go out and sit on the back porch. But not even that seemed to help, and for some reason he didn't even think it would do much good to talk it over with his father. It looked like he would just have to tough it out by himself, and he felt lonelier than he ever had before in his life.

Finally, after he had gone upstairs to go to bed, Tommy heard his parents in their room talking about the election. And his mother said again she didn't know why in the world Bob Dudley ever wanted to be county judge, he had enough to do anyway. But his father just said, well, maybe Bob just had to get the reformer complex out of his system and maybe now he could go back to work and practice law like he was supposed to do. And besides, he said, nobody on earth could have beaten Dr. Jennings, who, for all his lack of legal knowledge, *was* one of the most highly regarded men in the county and might know a lot more about *folks*, a lot more about the world than Bob Dudley, as fine a man and as dear a friend as he was. "You know," he said to Tommy's mother just before he rolled over and went to sleep, "ideals are all very well; but we all, in one way or another, whatever game we're playing, occasionally have to play politics too. And whether we like it or not, we have to remember that some wise man once defined *that* as 'the art of the possible.' "

The Peabody Ducks and All the Rest

"Come over here, son, and see the ducks in the fountain," my mother said. "It's high time you knew you and they had the same name. And you might even be kinfolks! You want to know what kind of duck it is? Well, I think it's a mallard, but it's also called a drake (since it's a male) so this makes it something for you to reckon with now and hereafter. And if you want to look at it in yet another way, it could also be related to the great Sir Francis Drake, who vowed to singe the king of Spain's beard. (Philip II, I believe.) And since you also have the same surname as these ducks right here, rejoice that you have that identity and be proud of it."

Then she went on to say that it was Sir Walter Raleigh rather than Sir Francis Drake who spread his cloak before the Queen to keep her feet from getting wet, and people were always able to tell them apart like that. But it was also Sir Francis who knelt before the queen on the *Golden Hind* so she could knight him right there on his own ship. And then when you got Leicester and Cecil and a few other noblemen into the game, you had a really glorious court. And the Armada was no match for them: all of them said the wind was in their favor at the time as it was later on for William of Orange (they called it a "Protestant" wind then) and also worked the same miracle much later for the English against Hitler at Dunkirk, which made for the largest headlines ever carried in the Memphis *Commercial Appeal*. Was it just luck or something more? Who could know? Suffice it to say that luck, magic, even grace—all sorts of things— may have been involved: it really didn't matter and maybe the English were just born lucky.

But I'm far off the track on all this. Anybody knows where I come from—west Tennessee, fifty miles north of Memphis. And he will know at once where this scene is all taking place—in the lobby of the Peabody Hotel. And the ducks—their white feathers brushed with green, had been there about as long as I had been alive. And after this I never forgot that we had a stout bond in our names, and it was something nobody could ever take away from any of us. But it wasn't like bragging on your kinfolks or trying to get into the DAR or some other honorary organization. For what it was worth, my father always said he wouldn't give you fifty cents for the whole kit and caboodle. And if you got so carried away by the mere idea of a "family tree," you'd better watch your step because you might find apes and God knows what else swinging around up there from limb to limb.

I believe the Peabody ducks were raised way up on the roof above us, and they were brought down every morning by some of the bellhops, installed in the pool surrounding the fountain, then taken back again to the roof late in the afternoon. They were very well trained too—rarely getting out of the pool, always looking elegant, if not courtly. And it was a sight to see that everybody visiting Memphis always took advantage of now, along with Graceland and the Hernando DeSoto Bridge, especially in the latter case, at night, gleaming across the River as it crossed over from Arkansas, and the West, maybe even the Pacific, holding our country, our whole world together in some very special way.

Tennessee and Arkansas were bound together especially fast, though in a way which might not have pleased the citizens of the latter: in making any kind of comparisons between the two, whether in the economy or in the public schools or something else, Tennesseans always said, "Thank God for Arkansas" because that guaranteed the existence of at least one other place in the world that was worse off than we were. (Of course we could have said "Thank God for Mississippi" too, but I think most of us thought the difference between those two was hardly worth making any stir about.) There *was* one more point of difference between us and the two others which was sometimes mentioned: you could get married in either of those states all in a minute even if you wanted to because there was

no waiting period for the marriage license (I don't think either of
them required a blood test beforehand), so it was usually over to
Marion, Arkansas, or down to Hernando, Mississippi, if you were in
a big hurry, especially when it was possible to refer to it later as a
"secretly" performed ceremony, with the date all set back in the
record to make it add up to the requisite number of months.

And among all these wonders there was also DeSoto himself
when he first arrived, viewing the Mississippi, along with his men
and assorted Indians, on a great mural in the lobby of the Gayoso
Hotel, where my mother and father had spent their honeymoon. And
of course nobody ever forgot that either—and especially the grandi-
ose lobby itself where some of Forrest's men had ridden in on their
horses, hoping to kidnap the Union commander who was staying
there during his occupation of the city.

But no, it wasn't a beautiful city. It was flat and not particularly
picturesque. And yet it had presence, character, and you knew what
it was and where it was the minute you set eyes on it, even more so
now that the River front had both Mud Island and the Pyramid on
display to bring it all up to date in modern times. And at the foot of
the bluff, which overlooked the river from Front Street, you could
feel the whole eastern half of the continent at your back, giving you
the strongest possible support as you looked out across the river to
the West and the setting sun and knew that the East was all behind
you, the established past supporting you with all its history as you
looked forward to whatever unknown wonders might lie ahead. It had
stayed that way too, as long as you or anybody else could remember,
and somehow, you felt, always would, just like the river itself. And
it was also that way with Main Street, which ran parallel to Front
Street, and also looked toward the river—the street where all the
cotton buyers had their offices and where the Cotton Exchange stood
at the corner of Union and Front too. (There's even a plaque
honoring John Grisham on that corner of the building now.)

Then, farther north, occupying a whole block between Main and
Second, there was Court Square, with a bandstand right in the

middle, along with lots of pigeons and other phenomena like band concerts and playing fountains which seemed magical too. And there was a bronze tablet on a formidable stone beside the bandstand in memory of Walter Malone, who had written the poem, "Opportunity," which was supposed, I think, to be a sort of inspirational incentive to help him quit drinking and thereby perfectly fill the role my mother's view of literature advocated—that it should forever be "uplifting." And it began with:

> They do me wrong who say I come no more
> When once I knock and fail to find you in;
> For every day I stand outside your door,
> And bid you wake, and rise to fight and win. . . .

He was a Mississippian by birth but spent most of his life in Tennessee, a judge of some distinction back around the turn of the century, but not without some sorrows: he never married and finally died of an apoplectic seizure in the Peabody Hotel.

Then the "avenues," which ran east and west as contrasted with the north and south "streets," making something of a checkerboard (all very flat of course) of the downtown area. Then the rest of the city spreading eastward, toward the universities, there to remain, through the Medical Center and the Central Gardens District, all waiting for something beautiful and fixed. And North, East, and South Parkway encircling it all, with a dark green boulevard, whose boundary in summer was formed by brilliant shrubbery and imposing magnolia trees. But for a bastion the West still had only the river.

Well, that was the center of its glamour, a little farther east from Midtown, with Overton Park and the Pink Palace, the latter a mansion named by Clarence Saunders, the automatic grocery king (he founded Piggly Wiggly), for its never-changing style—pink stone and always the same. And on out east—Central, Poplar—it stretched, past elegant suburbs—Germantown, Walnut Grove Road, and on and on. But as for Memphis north and south, of course nothing much but open fields and woods—and, alas, kudzu vines—connecting *them*.

Midtown and the East—they were its real center and of course nothing spreading westward and only flatter and flatter Mississippi to the South and its ultimate culmination, the Delta.

Nothing to be changed, any more than the Peabody and the ducks. Nothing of great charm, yet somehow inviting, waiting for what might be coming, wherever and whenever, but only that, somehow alluring in its very stability, even mystery. The downtown unchanging too—no Spanish moss, few camellias, only some fine old houses left there, still looking toward the river but nothing more. And, I thought, the more they thought they changed, the more they probably stayed the same.

But by the time I was grown the downtown department stores and picture shows were all gone too. Was that the story of the city itself? Would it be the same as with my own name then? Perhaps so. Indeed, what could you do with it—plain as it was, incapable of being either misspelled or mispronounced? I couldn't imagine any other future for it. Well then, what did it matter finally? Nothing that I could see, as long as it stayed put, but always itself, unchanging and unchanged.

All That Believe That, Stand on Their Head!

Every boy, then later on every man must have as a confidante about sexual and other delicate matters a woman who is not too close: his mother of course would never do. She would be too proprietary and—who knows?—maybe for the same reason that some psychiatrists say a father or a mother has always been reluctant to give children instruction about sex: it's just too close to something incestuous. And just for the record, his father or another man in the role would be no good: men—yes, *Southern* men too—are often more prudish than women and less realistic. For what it's worth, I never had one iota of information from either of my parents about anything to do with sex. And they only began alluding to it one day when I was about twelve and they woke up and realized that I already knew *something* about it, just about the same time they came to and acknowledged the fact that I had found out about Santa Claus.

Well, without getting into an argument about that, males can't know all they want—or need—to know about that fascinating other sex or anything appertaining thereunto on their own. (William Faulkner, again and again, implies that they simply don't know as much about most anything to do with *folks* as women anyhow. And thus the "initiations" most of his male characters have to undergo at some crucial point in their lives. The women of course can just sit on the front porch and find out all they need to know by osmosis.) But men do need to talk to somebody who knows and understands it; they have girl playmates when they're young, who often don't turn into "sweethearts" when they approach the years when the sap begins to rise. Such girls of course are great *chums* during high school and very good to work your algebra problems over the phone with every night but it never goes beyond that. Really, it's almost like a business deal. And when the young bucks are grown and the sap *has* risen with a vengeance, they still must have as an advisor somebody who isn't either a romantic interest or his wife and the mother of his children.

On both counts I've been lucky. As a boy, I had several close girl buddies—and that's exactly what they were too, buddies and chums, not girl friends; and as an adolescent—and on into adulthood—I had a beloved relative, called Auntee, whom I could ask anything and everything of and who certainly didn't mind *straightening me out*, as they say, on all matters of belief and action where she thought I might be going wrong. But when I was a boy, it was my con- temporary, Ann Louise Parker, who lived right up the street, and who was born knowing the relations that fundamentally existed between the sexes, though she didn't see or put them in explicitly sexual terms. (She also had several brothers and sisters, while I had none.) And like all women, young or old, then or now, she knew what the power structure was, where it lay and who manipulated it though she couldn't have put it in those terms.

But she was death on manners and *propriety*—how boys should act with girls: they should never take advantage of their female "weaknesses" (I never knew exactly what they were) and always treat them as "special" people who were somehow superior to boys, people who had to be handled with kid gloves at all times. But needless to say, I thought I could see the contradiction in all this: for me, such nomenclature and such treatment gave them some sort of shield to hide behind and put boys at a very unfair disadvantage. And when they proudly proclaimed that they were *ladies* and should always be treated as such, I sometimes made bold to reply that I treated people like ladies when they behaved like ladies. Even then I had a sense that this embodied something like one law for them and another for us, some sense of a double standard; and I thought it unfair. And like Auntee would have said about something she strongly doubted or objected to, I wanted to holler, loud and clear, "All that believe that, stand on their head!"

But like I said, as I grew up, I began to consult her more and more on such matters; and she was an authority of the first rank there. For one thing, she had been married to an old man—a widower who was old enough to be her father, raised his two sons by his first wife for him, then nursed him through a long final illness presided over by one of Memphis's finest, the great Dr. Livermore, whose very name was indeed a real pun because I've heard her remark many a time, "Why, child, that man taught me how to *live!*" And I think she really adored her husband too, though my father said that, though he came from nice folks, he really looked like—and probably was—a pretty rough customer, who probably abused her and was unfaithful on top of that. (One of the cousins even said there was a young boy on their farm—just a sharecropper too—who looked just like Auntee's husband.) And after he finally died, way up in his eighties, there was nothing for Auntee, who had always been a sort of poor relation, to do but go back to live with the two old-maid sisters, Cousin Rosa and Cousin Emma, who had more or less raised her, and then in due course nurse *them* through their final illnesses and bury them after they had gone on to what one of my old friends called the larger life. But then he was an ex-Methodist turned into an Episcopalian, and a former Democrat who had forsaken his traditional heritage for the Republican Party. And my father said, well, what else could you expect?

But before Auntee first came back to live with the cousins, she went to work downtown at Kroger's, to see how she would like being more her own boss and manager and not completely at the old maids' beck and call. But it didn't take long for her to realize that the atmosphere down there would be considerably different in shadow and substance from that up at the two sisters'; and before long she would decide that, for all its constraints, she would probably be more comfortably, indeed more properly settled up there. Anyhow, when she first began working down at Kroger's, she was at one of the cash registers, checking people out. And since she had always had a glad hand and a smiling face for everybody, she continued doing so then, and I should have thought she would have been a great asset to the business in that post. But when a rather grim and greasy woman with crossed eyes came through the line one day with a whole passel of mixed goods—fruit, vegetables, meat, flour, staples, the whole lot, Auntee looked up, smiled, and said, as she was putting it all through the register, "Why, this is certainly miscellaneous, isn't it?" But the woman, without a smile or even batting a single one of her crossed eyes, replied simply, "No, ma'am, it's Mrs. Peacock." But mistress of manners that she was, Auntee could think of nothing to say but, "Well, I declare. . . ."

A bit later, after they had moved her back to the meat market (did they fear her natural talent for public relations was going *too* far with the clientele?), old Mrs. Sunderman, who was deaf as a post and nosy into the bargain, stopped in front of the meat counter one day and pointed to a tray of what were often referred to delicately as Rocky Mountain oysters and asked Horace Lee Lightfoot, the butcher, what they were, whereupon he shouted, for all the customers to hear, "Hog nuts!" But she wasn't to be put down by anything so harmless as that, so she drew herself up with great dignity, clucked her tongue and set him to rights with "You ought to be ashamed of yourself." And Auntee said everybody in the store burst out laughing because the two combatants were known to one and all and they regarded the whole thing as a draw pure and simple. But she said *she* had had about enough of the salt-of-the-earth element, the hog-and-hominy crowd, and decided she would just go back to Cousin Rosa and Cousin Emma's and retire into genteel quietude.

My mother said God knew she had her work cut out for her up there because they were both of them spoiled rotten and generally helpless about dealing with the big wide world. Cousin Rosa had taught the first grade in Woodville for nearly fifty years, and Cousin Emma managed her—and the housekeeping—like it was all a matter of teaching the first grade too. But she herself had something of an escape hatch: she had *enjoyed poor health* for a good many years— after her one and only beau had eloped with the daughter of the county's main bootlegger. They said the young girl's father kept his "stock" nailed up in the wall of his living room; but, in any case, he had the manners of a perfect gentleman, a regular Chesterfield. And the groom soon took his bride off to Texas to live, and it wasn't any time before they struck oil on the small ranch he had bought. And everybody said, well, that just went to show you, but they never did say *what*.

Anyhow, it was shortly after that that Cousin Emma had had a "nervous breakdown" and afterwards, as she herself admitted, was never "really strong." But she had the determination and the persistence of William Lloyd Garrison, who proclaimed when he founded his fire-eating abolitionist journal, "I am in earnest—I will not equivocate—I will not excuse—I will not retreat a single inch; and I will be heard!" and naturally assumed that whatever ailed her was of supreme importance to all her friends and neighbors, to say nothing of the kinfolks. One time I remember she even called up my mother just to tell her she had "one of those old-fashioned sick headaches" and was just suffering *death*. But unfortunately, my mother was downtown, so I had to take—and relay—the message.

This wasn't quite as dramatic as the time we all went on a trip up to the Smoky Mountains in Cousin Rosa's little blue Ford she had just bought and, at the age of seventy, was *determined* to learn to drive. But fortunately for all and sundry, my mother's brother, who had worked for the state highway department before he retired, was at the wheel and everybody said he knew all the roads *like the back of his hand*. Nevertheless, Cousin Rosa got, as she put it, "most gloriously carsick" from all those hairpin curves; and every time she lifted up her head to see whether she was still alive, there would be a sign beside the road saying "Prepare to Meet Thy God" or "Jesus Is Coming Soon." But somehow I thought Cousin Emma really won hands down because she would simply announce from time to time, apropos of nothing, that her head was just *aching* with constipation!

Anyhow, I think everybody in town knew that Cousin Rosa and Cousin Emma got along much better than they pretended and somehow really *enjoyed* their ups and downs. (My mother said, of course they did: it all gave them something to do.) But the two of them finally died and left Auntee everything they had, so she was "well fixed" and everybody was glad because they said if mortal had ever *earned* an inheritance, she had. And they hoped now she would kick up her heels and enjoy it all before she herself got too old.

And I think she did, though she did acknowledge that she had had lots of "tough luck" beforehand. For one thing, she had never had to fool with—or put up with—ornery domestic help. And when Miss Mattie Caldwell up the street, who was her dearest friend, had to have a live-in practical nurse during her last illness, she spoke out loud and bold when she heard "that woman" they had up there staying with her was "just not of the right calibre" and had men calling her up in the middle of the night and all sorts of cute things going on. And she said she was just going to have to speak to Miss Mattie's son, Walter Jr., about it all because they didn't *have* to put up with anything like that. And the Lord knew that, even with all the folks she herself had nursed and buried, she never had to either: she said she never yet had had a wench in *her* house.

Well, this was all the sort of thing we talked about when I would go up to her house late in the evening to wash my clothes. Of course the aunt and uncle with whom I stayed when I visited back home had a perfectly good washer and dryer, but you couldn't sit there and really *talk* to them about anything, certainly not folks or even the news of the day, to say nothing of matters of what you might call faith and morals. To tell the truth, I don't think either one of them really enjoyed idle talk or gossip. For one thing, my aunt came from a very large and very "close" family: she had more than thirty first cousins right there in Woodville—one of the first families in our town, as they would have been the first to tell you. So that automatically insured that some of the best tales there couldn't be told in *their* house. (Of course the main thing in her life had always been family—first, last, and always.) And as if explaining her disinclination for trivial and amusing conversation or the open and public display of affection (what you might call the "comfortable" things), she would always say hers had never been a "demonstrative" family. And anyway, everybody knew she just didn't have the narrative gift: "I never could tell a story," she would say. And I always wanted to ask her whether she was bragging or complaining.

My uncle (who had been my father's younger brother) usually didn't have much to say either: I think he believed idle talk was just a waste of time. He was not without a sense of humor, though; but it was, more likely than not, inclined toward the sardonic, which of course was not very comfortable when it was directed at you. And as I've already observed, I think he regarded talk, unless it was somehow connected with the bank where he worked and its affairs, as somehow of no importance. On the other hand, he did sometimes speak with approbation of old Dr. Steele, who, he said, got rich by not talking; and my mother said maybe so because his patients could get well or die and be resurrected but he hadn't said yet what was wrong with them.

So maybe my uncle thought *silence* was something valuable, like money in the bank, while *talking* was too much like being a spend-thrift—"running through everything you had in no time at all," as people often put it. On the whole, I later came to think, he and my aunt were both chary with many things that brought joy into life. And I could hardly understand their attitude: it certainly wasn't like Auntee's or that of many others whom I loved. Now I think I must even then have agreed with Jane Austen's Mr. Bennet, when he remonstrates with his daughter Elizabeth by asking her why else we live except to make sport for our neighbors and then laugh at them in our turn. But I did know that people who "didn't talk" usually made me sad.

Like I said, these were the times—late at night when I was doing my laundry—when Auntee and I would do our talking, exchanging the news of the day and of course, always, the news of *folks* because of course that was what all news was finally about. It was also the time when we indulged in our little venture into wickedness—a shot

or two of Jack Daniel's or J&B, which I must say Auntee took a
great liking to. God knows what Cousin Rosa and Cousin Emma
would have thought, much less said, about such behavior in their
house—or my uncle and aunt, for that matter. Cousin Rosa, as a strict
Baptist teetotaler, would have been scandalized: there's no other word
for it. But I suspect Cousin Emma, herself a Methodist but a rather
lukewarm one, might not have minded going along for the ride, like
she almost literally did that time at the Chicago World's Fair (the one
that was called "the Century of Progress") when she went on an
excursion up to Milwaukee, one of whose "sights" to be seen was
one of the great breweries. (And of course its wares were to be
sampled too.)

Cousin Emma had always said she would try anything once, so
when they got there, she jumped off the bus along with the rest of
the party—all but a woman who sat there looking like she had just
swallowed a ramrod and, on top of that, had eaten too many prunes
and they had all settled in her face. And Cousin Emma said she had
"WCTU" written all over her; but she just said to herself, "*There's
Miss Rosa*" and went on her way. She didn't think much of the beer,
though; but she said she would always be glad she had given it a try
because now she wouldn't have to worry the rest of her life wondering what it tasted like.

You might say that Cousin Emma, unlike Cousin Rosa, was a
real pragmatist—just like the time Cousin Rosa was going out to
Arizona for her asthma and, as they were crossing the desert, the air-
conditioning in the Pullman car went off and all the passengers were
sweltering away and the conductor came back and invited them all to
go up to the club car just ahead, where he said they would be perfectly comfortable. But Cousin Rosa declined: *she* wasn't about to go
up there, where all she could do was just sit there for the next couple
of hours watching the other passengers *swilling beer*. But when she
told Cousin Emma about this little episode on returning home, Cousin
Emma just snorted and told her if she didn't have any more sense
than that, she deserved to stay back in the Pullman and burn up alive.

But to get back to Auntee and what I more or less learned from her, perhaps the most memorable of her "lessons" came when I voiced my dissatisfaction with the differences between the way men and women were treated when they "misbehaved," whether in fiction or in life. (That was certainly the way it was in a small town like Woodville or in the *Ladies' Home Journal*, for that matter.) When they were talking about a boy, people just usually said "well, boys will be boys" or "young men just have to sow their wild oats" or something of the sort; but women were severely criticized, even at times held in disgrace. And, as an adolescent, I didn't understand it and thought it very unfair. But not Auntee, who when I asked her why this was, spoke out with great conviction, "Well, you see, Baby [which she always called me as long as she lived], men are *weak*; and if it weren't for women upholding the moral standards of the community, we just wouldn't have any!" And I thought for a minute she was going to add, "And all that believe otherwise, stand on their head!"—her usual way of making assurance double sure. But instead, she just cleared her throat, pulled her girdle down, and forthrightly tucked her brassiere inside her neckline as if daring it to give her any trouble any time soon. I wasn't sure just what that all settled, but it was clear that she intended for what she had said to be taken that way. Like they said when the pope made a pronouncement on faith and morals, there was no more now to be said on the subject. And thus the Victorian double standard came into my life though I still didn't know exactly what it was all about. But something fierce and final; I felt perfectly sure of that.

Well, as I heard many people say later on, there were many *positive* characters back in those days; and what they *said*, they usually *meant*. And their word was usually *yea* or *nay*, and always you were told that *their word was their bond*. I suppose it almost had to be that way, given the uncertain state of the world and the times. And believing or saying that something patently false was true was certainly flirting with the world, the flesh, and the devil, even taking chances with the Almighty and making a bigger fool out of yourself than need be or the Lord intended. That was certain. So you might as well take things as they were, make the best of them, and swallow them whole, like a good dose of medicine. Like my mother always said, such things always made you stronger. In any case, that way you could maintain your dignity and your credibility and always be considered by everybody *a man among men.* In any case, you certainly wouldn't have to stand on your head.

A Short Horse

The last thing Miss Lucy Cobb did every night before she went to bed was brush her hair a hundred strokes, read a chapter in the Bible, and write a letter to her daughter, Lois, who lived up north in Detroit. A lot of times she couldn't think of anything *new* to tell her, but it just seemed a good habit—to stay in touch with her only daughter on a regular basis. Of course when the dial telephones came in, Lois started calling her mother regularly: it cost only a dollar for three minutes, she said. But Miss Lucy said anything she had to say Lois could wait a couple of days to hear unless it was the direst kind of emergency, in which case she would have called her anyhow. You could love somebody more than anything in the world, she said, but you didn't have to act a fool about it. And of course the old saying was right—that a short horse was soon curried—but then Lois always was something of a boss and manager and inclined to be quick on the trigger too; but she said she had always known that.

Her sister-in-law, Miss Carrie, who lived next door, was different, though. She didn't brush *her* hair every night, and she certainly didn't read a chapter out of the Bible. Such a rigid discipline wasn't conducive to sleep, she said. And when she wanted to write *her* daughter, Mary Jane, it would be because she had something important to say and not just on principle. And besides, Mary Jane or "Sister," as she usually called her, wasn't just a mere housewife, like Lois; she was having a *career* as a buyer in a big department store in Memphis. And that carried a lot of responsibility with it; and she hadn't even had time to get married yet, much less stay in touch with her mother almost constantly. Besides, she and Mary Jane had always thought alike about most things; and she didn't think they *needed* to stay in touch that often. But once when she made a point of saying something of the sort to Miss Lucy, Miss Lucy had just calmly replied that, well, it just depended on the way you were raised and how you looked at things and everybody had his—or her—own ideas about that. And that seemed to settle the matter for both of them.

Still, there was never any open disagreement between the two ladies: it was more like an armed truce most of the time. And their husbands, who were brothers, had always managed to stay on reasonable terms with each other despite occasional differences about the farmland they owned together. Nevertheless, according to Miss Carrie, there was no doubt that while Miss Lucy was something of a cool and collected lady, to say nothing of a well disciplined one, she wasn't any Goody Two-Shoes by a long shot and wasn't nearly as innocent as she looked. In fact, she was once even heard to refer to Miss Lucy's "seeming innocence."

But then she herself, as she said everybody knew, was something of a go-getter (able to handle a short horse?) and didn't let the grass grow under *her* feet about anything any time. And Miss Lucy herself acknowledged as much: she had always told her children—Lois and the two boys—that Aunt Carrie could do just about *anything*. And always Dick-in-a-minute about getting things done *now*, whatever the case; and when time came to cut the head off, she was right there to do it. There was no doubt about it: she was a very capable woman.

But perhaps, she sometimes thought, she had overreached herself once when Lois was about ten and one day hollered in from the back yard (from where she usually chose to broadcast any delicate items so the whole neighborhood could hear) that she had just thought of one thing Aunt Carrie couldn't do: she couldn't *sing*. Whereupon Miss Carrie, who had been weeding out the flower bed on her own side of the fence, suddenly rose up in view, cleared her throat, and primly announced that well, she never had tried. But no, there really wasn't anything to fall out about: it was just symptomatic of the differences between the two women, was all. They both—and everybody else—knew that. And so nobody took offense.

For that matter, Lois and Mary Jane themselves stayed on very good terms with each other, though the differences between their respective mothers were sometimes all too visible in the two of them. One thing was that Mary Jane sometimes seemed to act on sheer caprice, with no rhyme or reason, at least not that anybody knew about. Like for instance the time when, without saying a word to Miss Carrie, she had changed music teachers, casting aside Mrs. Owen, who was an especially good friend of her mother's if somewhat too much wedded to convention in art as well as in life (her recitals had all the precision of military drills) and ran off after Mrs. Parsons, who people said was always up to snuff and a pinch over but, to the chagrin—and perhaps satisfaction—of Miss Carrie, eventually, as she remarked to somebody, "took all the rhythm out of Sister."

But then, if you looked at it that way, Mrs. Parsons herself had enough rhythm to last both her *and* her pupils the rest of their lives: why, when she sat down at the piano, everybody said she could really make that thing talk. She was just that quick on the trigger, you might say, about everything else. (Perhaps she too would have made short work of currying the short horse.) Everybody in town knew that, in addition to her piano classes, she made a very good thing out of raising chickens and selling eggs on the side but was also known on occasion to have sent a customer who had ordered a dozen eggs only eleven because, she said, one of them had a double yolk.

But her pupils were all *devoted* to her, it was said. Why, every day at recess the "Owenites" and the "Parsonians," as they called themselves, used to get in a fight of some sort—no insignia of course but each one signifying his or her allegiance by squinching up his nose if he was on Mrs. Owen's "side" (she had a pronounced "Roman" nose) or hollering the battle cry for Mrs. Parsons with a pronounced stutter, which that good lady had had all her life.

Lois of course didn't worry about things like that at all; and she intended to be quite happy when she got out of high school and went on to the Normal in Memphis to get a teacher's certificate, whereas Mary Jane, largely at her mother's instigation, was headed for Ward-Belmont in Nashville, which some people thought was just a society school where girls went to get polished off—"finished," as they put it—and catch husbands from among the rich young men who went to Vanderbilt. On the other hand, Lois never had seemed to care about appearances or how things *looked*. But then neither she nor Mary Jane was going to fall out with the other over just a matter of *taste*.

It was all a matter of keeping your feet on the ground, apparently. And in that respect there was no doubt where the two mothers, much less their daughters, stood. When Mary Jane, one summer during the depths of the Depression, married a salesman whom she had met in the course of her work in the department store (unfortunately, it was reported that he "traveled in ladies' underwear"), nothing would do but she—or Miss Carrie—had to have a professionally prepared wedding cake (three-tiered, with bride and groom on top of course) along with all the other trimmings though she did forego having a real live florist in to decorate the church but instead relied mainly on her friends and lots of Queen Anne's lace they found growing out in the cow pastures and along the country roads.

On the other hand, when, some years later, Lois stepped off with a young engineer who, for a wedding trip, immediately took her off to Australia, where he was being sent by his company to install some turbines, she took along her latest homemade evening dress to wear at dinner on the ship but, when asked, told everybody that no, it hadn't been made by one of the great French designers like Chanel or Schiaparelli but by "Marcelline," though she didn't add that that was the local seamstress, Marcelline Higgins, who everybody at home said had a "wicked way" with a pair of scissors as well as being more than able to cast a wide net for every good looking man that came down the pike. But then, like Marcelline, Lois could always improvise, and everybody knew from that that she was certainly going to "make" a good teacher.

And that's perhaps what she had sought to prove that time, before she married, when Miss Lucy was having such a problem with one of her pupils in the fifth-grade class at the Methodist Sunday school. Tom Frank Childress just didn't seem to *want* to respond to the Bible stories she told them, certainly not "spiritually." And if there was any way to turn one of them into a joke, he would avail himself of the opportunity right on the spot, like asking whether the whale that swallowed Jonah was able to *digest* him and why Lot's wife didn't get turned into something more appetizing than a pillar of salt, which he certainly didn't think was very bright. And Miss Lucy couldn't seem to get anywhere with him with her usual "gentle" touch. (As she said, she just couldn't "reach" him.)

Obviously, stronger methods were needed—and perhaps a short horse or even the two bears that had disposed so effectively of the children who made fun of Elisha. And apparently Lois, who in many ways was not her mother's child for nothing, was prepared to apply something of the sort. Because she told her mother she would be glad to lend her a hand in "straightening out" Tom Frank or anybody else that needed it. (My own mother said at the time that that wouldn't do any good. People like Tom Frank—and the whole Childress family, for that matter—never had had much sense to begin with and were everyone of them almost too lazy to breathe—and to wake them up from their long slumber, only to apprise them of what they had been left out of all along, would be downright cruelty.)

But anyhow one Sunday before long, Lois announced to her mother that she herself would teach the class for her that day and when Miss Lucy introduced her, she could tell the children that the lesson for that Sunday would be about a seeing-eye dog. Now what all that had to do with the Christian religion I don't suppose Miss Lucy or anybody else ever quite knew; but it all seemed like a worthy cause and a serious issue, overflowing with kindness and concern, right up there with Helen Keller and Florence Nightingale.

And at first that Sunday morning matters seemed to be going the right way: Lois might really be successful in stemming the tide of levity if not downright impudence (all of it not a thing in the world but just the Old Adam) that had been running so high. And right off the bat she had steamed in on Tom Frank, putting the matter to him that blindness was a terrible thing, maybe the most "lonesome" affliction of all. People who were *normal*, "like most of us," she said, just couldn't imagine what it would be like—to be helpless and completely dependent on others for assistance with almost everything. But, miraculously, somebody somewhere had discovered that these wonderful dogs, when properly trained, were capable of supplying all sorts of help in such circumstances to the "unsighted"—things that might make the difference literally between life and death if it came to that. And how would *he*, Tom Frank, feel then about such a friend and companion? How would he treat him, what would he *do* for him? And of course his prompt response was "Beat him!" At which the whole class immediately dissolved into laughter, all except Miss Lucy and, I suspect, Lois, who may well have wondered what she had wrought and whether or not there were some situations where a short horse wasn't exactly what was called for. And that was that.

Had Lois been hoist with her own petard, had she outsmarted herself? Miss Lucy (out of policy or partiality?) would never comment except to tell somebody one time years later that anybody that wanted to get ahead of Tom Frank Childress would have to get up early and go to bed late. Why, just look at him right that minute, she said—running a roadhouse out on the Memphis highway but, she understood, never missing a meeting of Alcoholics Anonymous! And besides, everybody with any sense at all ought to have realized years ago that anybody who could make people laugh at the very *idea* of a seeing-eye dog, to say nothing of wooden legs and glass eyes, obviously had talents that were—mercifully—denied most other folks in this world. In some ways, she said, you really had to hand it to him. He might be a short horse, but he wasn't going to be curried any time soon.

Shrouds with Pockets in Them

I've always thought that of all the virtues, thrift can be the least attractive, even something of an opposite number to laziness, which has always seemed to me that most repulsive of all the sins. Stinginess with money, food, all that sort of thing is bad enough; but what seems mainly off-putting about thrift is that it can run so much to just plain low-down selfishness—which for me covers it all, whether it's giving of your wealth and substance or just being unwilling to give of yourself, to put out, as we say, for anybody else in the world.

And I'm sorry to say my greatest exposure to that comes from members of my own family—a cousin, in particular, who didn't think he had to do anything but just take a seat on the front porch and wait for good luck or the grace of God or something of the sort to drive up and blow the horn. And then whatever it was that was coming his way—without any effort of his own—would just fall out of the sky into his lap. And naturally, people like that always thought they deserved it just because they always thought they did—in his case because he was the son of a Methodist circuit rider and had grown up the "hard way" and therefore, it seemed, was planning to devote the rest of his life to complaining about the things he had never had and the opportunities he had missed. And I found out, along the way, that most people like that had rather die than say "please" or "thank you" because, I think, in some way that would indicate that they felt some sort of obligation to *somebody* and would thus owe somebody else for a change rather than, though they wouldn't admit it, the other way around.

I remember when I was about in the third grade, this particular cousin came to live with us while he worked in my father and uncle's hardware store. Whether he paid board or not I don't know; I imagine it was just included as part of his salary, which couldn't have been much in those Depression days. But anyhow, I had to give up my room, which had always been called the guest room (I wondered sometimes whether my parents thought I was just a visitor in the house) and move into their own bedroom, where they slept in the double bed in which I had been born; and I slept across the room from them on what used to be called a daybed—a sort of halfway between a single and a double size which I remembered my mother taking naps on in the daytime and where she always did her reading for "pleasure," which meant whatever reading she did other than the newspaper, usually her "club" books, which were always handed on to the one next in line when it met twice a month. (I well remembered her reading parts of *Gone With the Wind* to me while she was stretched out there and I was supposed to be having my afternoon nap in the double bed.)

I think I had sense enough even then to know this was not a good thing, even before I had ever heard anything of Dr. Freud. My parents had no privacy and I didn't either, and I remember swearing to myself that if I ever did grow up, there were two things I would have, no matter what—a bedroom of my own and one with a fire in it too, so I wouldn't have to get as warm as I could stand it in my parents' room before the fire in the grate, then running across the hall to the "guest" room and jumping in between the ice-cold sheets and have my teeth start chattering before I could even get off to sleep. As it was, after my cousin came to live with us, even he had to sleep in that unheated room and sometimes, if it was cold enough, come into the other bedroom where my parents and I slept and dress before the fire there. And somehow I didn't think that was a very good thing either.

Well, even though my cousin had been raised "harder" than I had (it hardly needs saying that Methodist circuit riders made very little money back then), it didn't keep him from being "peculiar," which of course always means selfish and, incidentally, extravagant because of the burden it puts on other people. And so there he was, with my mother making delicious biscuits and rolls for every meal, always having to have a small plate of Wonder Bread beside his dinner plate because, for some reason known only to God, that's what he had come to prefer in his young adulthood. The thought of it makes me want to gag even now, and I think his attitude was probably based on his delusion that anything made by hand, at home was bound not to be so "fine" as something "modern" and manufactured by machines. *Our* bread was deliberately "unrefined," with all the good wholesome stuff still in it—the vitamins and the "roughage," as my mother called it. But the kind he preferred was always of course absolutely snow white and "pure." (And for what it's worth, I can tell you that he always ate loads of Kellogg's All-Bran for breakfast.)

I used to wonder at the time whether he thought such a preference about his bread indicated that he had come up in the world. And I remember thinking about him years later the first time I went to Russia and tasted their superb bread, so dark it was almost black and you could really think the Bible was right when it called it the staff of life; but then I thought, no, he wouldn't have liked that either, just probably looked on it as a holdover from the time of Czarist oppression—and fit only for peasants—or another Communist stratagem to undermine the health and morals of the West. Needless to say, he never, when he rose from the table at the end of a meal, thanked my mother for what he had eaten or even said that he had enjoyed it. And I wonder whether he thought that demeaning too. In any case, he wasn't giving anything away.

One more thing, and then I'll have done. My cousin was always careful to keep his hair slicked firmly down with Vitalis hair oil, which of course left a big greasy spot on the back of every high-backed chair he sat in. So my mother was compelled to put small hand towels (didn't we have any antimacassars?) on the back of them, but somehow some of the Vitalis always managed to seep through. And I wonder now how she put up with it all, but she was loyal always to my father and his family (the cousin was his nephew). And she wouldn't have considered any alternative. But it took its toll on her: he wasn't a real boarder yet he wasn't a real guest and with such an undefined status it was hard to know exactly how to treat him and where he belonged. But my mother being the way she was, I don't know that she ever spoke to my father about any of this. I think she just regarded it as her duty, and that was that.

(After my father was dead and the cousin was married and had become fairly prosperous in the feed business, my mother did open her mind on some of this to me on my rare visits back home and I found out she hadn't suffered all these things gladly, just bottled them up to draw interest, you might say, when her own judgment day arrived, though I'm not sure it ever really came. After all, she was first and foremost a *lady*. But at least I knew how she felt, and for her that was enough.)

But despite my distaste, my cousin and his ways used to fascinate me. For one thing, I never could figure out what his motives were. Was he just close with his money (he would never discuss it with you but had an insatiable curiosity about your own finances) and his sentiments (I never yet heard him tell anybody he loved him, not even his parents) because he had been raised "hard"? Had he had to do without so much, in the way of advantages and so on, that he was afraid to give—anything? One of his favorite *apologias* was "Of course I never had the opportunity to do *that*" . . . whatever it was. And I wondered whether he was taking some sort of revenge on you for supposedly having been "privileged," as we say now. In those days people just said "spoiled," no matter whether you had been ruined by too much, too soon or had just simply had lots of "opportunities," of which you took as much advantage as possible.

Anyhow, it was all an unattractive characteristic and certainly not one inclined to win friends and influence people. Certainly, not a way to make yourself popular. What could he *mean* in all this? It was—and still remains after all these years—something of a mystery. I had often wished for an older brother—someone to "look up to" and confide in, more nearly my own age than my parents. But I knew right off he wasn't having any of that. So finally I just left him alone; surely he wasn't going to live with us forever.

And he didn't. A few years after he moved in with us World War
II broke out, but it didn't seem to affect him very much. He spent
nearly four years doing office work in the quartermaster corps down
at a base somewhere on the Gulf Coast and of course never did get
shot at or have to shoot anybody else. And just about all he ever said,
when he signed off in his letters to my father and uncle, was that he
had to go to bed and catch up on his sleep. There certainly didn't
seem anything threatening or even exciting about any of that. Finally,
after the end of the war with Germany and Japan, he was discharged
and returned home, but not to live with us any more but with his
parents, who had now retired to Woodville. I was about to graduate
from high school and getting ready to go off to college, so I didn't
see as much of him anymore. And that was all right too. But I still
wondered about him from afar because I just never had known
anybody like that before. And I wondered whether there were many
people in the world like him.

I had thought he might never get married: maybe he just wasn't
cut out for loving or sharing anything. But I was wrong there because
a year or two later he began to court a young woman who had moved
to town from up the road somewhere to teach in the high school, and
he did it with a good deal of earnestness too—like this was something that was on his program and something you *ought* to do and he
meant to go on and get it done right then and there and get it over
with. It certainly didn't seem like a romantic view of the married
state to me—more like you were just checking it off the list. And
when I got to know his wife, I felt I hadn't been too far wrong; it
seemed pretty much a case of like marrying like. Because she wasn't
any more "forthcoming" than he was—just taught school all day—
"social studies, naturally"—and then went home and cooked supper
and went to bed. And that was about it.

No children of course, but then I never had expected them to
have any: that would have involved *putting yourself out* for somebody else. And I didn't think that would suit either one of them.
Somehow for them everything was all mostly getting by on the least

possible expenditure of energy and affection in whatever you did, leaving you mostly locked up inside your own skin and blind and deaf to everything else. If anybody else wanted to take them inside his life, that was strictly up to him: *they* were certainly not making the effort. They didn't even entertain, friends or family, to amount to anything. Again, that was effort, that was money. And if you ever did venture to entertain *them*, they wanted to pay their own way so, presumably, you wouldn't expect them to return your hospitality in due course.

Naturally, they were there every time the church door opened, for both morning and evening services on Sunday, and Wednesday prayer meetings too. And many were the ones who thought them a model of piety and decorum. And so they rocked along for a good many years until they reached their sixties and then both retired at once: he said he couldn't *wait* to retire and even she, never one for much conversation, said of their new state, that it wasn't so bad. And now they spent most of their days working in the yard or doing repairs around the house, though the burden of the latter fell mostly on him. (He told somebody that she had a long list of chores for him to do by the time he got out of bed every morning.) And again, I wondered what their life was all about.

I guess for me the bottom line, as we would now say, was that they didn't seem to have any *joy*; I never saw either of them make a spontaneous gesture of affection toward anyone, family or friends. What did life mean to them? And as time went on, with me having graduated from college, then moving to another part of the country to live and work, I still wondered, but from afar, which was all right too. It was still a mystery, and I thought perhaps it was just as well that they didn't have any children. Ever cautious, ever careful, and always tightfisted, they never took chances on anything; in short, they never gave, they never put out. Did they really think they were going to take it all with them in the end—money, love, whatever it might be? Was that what life was all about? And from time to time I often wondered what their fate would be.

* * *

As it turned out, it was one neither I—nor anybody else—could ever have predicted or foreseen. And the truth of the whole matter didn't emerge until some time afterward. Because one Sunday when they arrived back home from church right after noon, there was a rather scruffy looking young man lounging against their mailbox— out on the edge of town where they lived. And without a by-your-leave he asked them if they would be good enough to drive him over to the next county seat going east—Crockett City, it was—so he could catch the next bust for Nashville. And without further ado, they told him to get in the back seat, along with his duffel bag, and they would drive him the twenty miles over there. The last thing in the world I would ever have expected from them, not only on the grounds of thrift but also of caution. I had finally realized the *risk* of any kind was for them intolerable, and I'm still somewhat puzzled by the whole affair. Had they recently had some sort of revelation; or did they think, just for once, they might try something new, something different, even *exciting*?

Anyhow, a good deal of what follows is based on conjecture and police records. But almost as soon as they got well out of town, the young man, who told them he had just been discharged from the service and was trying to save his money by hitchhiking home to East Tennessee, pulled a gun on them, then ordered them off the main road down a country lane, where he proceeded systematically to shoot and kill them both, then threw their bodies in the ditch beside the road and drove off with the car. And nobody would ever have been the wiser hadn't the highway patrol hauled him in for speeding shortly thereafter, when of course the car was identified and the whole tale came out of the young man himself—who, it turned out, was only sixteen and no more a newly discharged veteran than a spook, mainly just a high school dropout, ready to kill or steal anybody or anything just so he could get somewhere else, it didn't matter where.

Really, it was all just too sad: that was the general view all over town. That fine, upstanding couple who had never hurt anybody in their lives and worked hard and saved their money and done right always—and now this . . . death at the hands of what almost seemed pure evil, no rhyme nor reason to any of it. It all just made you stop and think, they said. But in any case, one thing was certain: they didn't take anything with them, any more than the murderer did, when all was said and done. (At least *he* got life imprisonment, which was more than they did.) And one old man who spent most of his time every day sitting in the courthouse yard watching the world go by was even heard to observe that he didn't know what the world was coming to: not a one of the three, he said, seemed to realize that they never had made shrouds with pockets in them. And, good or bad, that's what it all came down to in the end.

How Come You Reckon He Did That?

One of my old-maid cousins used to polish off or sum up whatever there was in any situation which you just couldn't figure out by saying, "Well, he (or she) was a curious mortal, and there's just no point in trying to reckon whatever in the world made him (or her) do that." Sometimes just to make a long story short, she would just haul off and say "How come you reckon he did that?" But the meaning was just the same except for being a little more businesslike, a little more urgent. And of course, that never settled anything, but we lived in a small town, and people who come from places like that always want to know the whys and wherefores of anything the least bit irregular because they come into the world believing that there is always a *reason* for everything—and of course a *story* behind everything that happens. And of course it's certainly of the utmost importance to them because their respective hometowns are all of them more or less the center of the universe as far as they are concerned.

And whether you liked it or not, the world did make sense, though of course it was often easier to make believe that it didn't and thus get yourself excused from ever being responsible for anything. But yes, for them, somehow everything that happened was connected to everything else or, like a character in one of Robert Penn Warren's novels says, the whole world was like a gigantic spiderweb and if you touched just one filament there, however lightly, the whole thing would vibrate and thus alert the spider, who of course would have his venom all ready for you. In any case, whatever you did would be noticed by your neighbors or the government, even people on the other side of the world, to say nothing of God—it didn't matter. And you never really got away with anything. And "nothing is ever lost," he concluded—past, present, or future, for that matter.

But somehow I always wanted to think there would be some sort of explanation available especially if you died and went to Heaven; surely, God wouldn't just leave you dangling like that and, if nothing else, God would want you to know why some people went to Heaven and others went elsewhere. Or else what was the point of it all? But of course you knew that God was in complete charge "up there" and would run it all just like He intended anyway. But you did want to know *why*. Come on, tell the truth now: we were *all* "curious mortals" in one way or another, and we did want to know what mysterious things, people included, were all about, even if sometimes curiosity did kill the cat.

And of course there's no place like a small town to whet your appetite for such things, where everybody knows everybody else and you don't dare open your mouth about most anything till you've had a chance to look around the room and see who's there. Why, one of my aunts (by marriage, I'm happy to say), had nearly two dozen first cousins living right there and, on top of that, two uncles who ended up spending a couple of years as guests of the U.S. government in Atlanta because they got their hands in the bank till once too often. And one of them (the one that was always so oily) was even superintendent of the Baptist Sunday school! (I was scared of the other one because he was stout and baldheaded and always looked like he was mad about something, sort of like a bulldog.) And later, after I had read a lot of detective stories, I concluded that maybe they were what you called a "hard and soft team," where one policeman tried to give you the "gentle" approach during his turn at giving you the third degree ("now, son, I've got a boy at home the same age you are . . . ") while the other didn't give a damn about that but just stood by ready at a moment's notice to beat the bejesus out of you with a baseball bat.

Of course the matter of "kinnery" or who's kin to whom can always be a dangerous thing to handle if you don't know your way around, but that *is* one thing small towns are good at. I know one time one of the lady deans at the university where I teach got "let go" because she didn't realize the professor whom she had, after her usual fashion, more or less insulted was the daughter of a state senator. I of course would have known that in a minute, but city folks seem to take pride in their ignorance of such matters. ("Why, I don't know a single one of the other renters in my apartment house!")

But as for the *reason* the two bankers went astray, who knew the answer to that? I know one of my father's friends said, well, they really hadn't *meant* to do anything wrong, just got involved in a precarious financial situation, maybe trusted people too much or made some bad loans—something like that; and the harder they tried to get out of it, the more firmly they were caught—just like quicksand. But my father wasn't having any of that. He said everybody in this world that had any sense knew the difference between right and wrong and there was just no use trying to pretend otherwise, human nature being what it was. And, if you had any doubt about it, all you needed to do was just look in the mirror.

And furthermore, there was no wiggling out of it either. The brother of the bulldog man, who was a big-time operator in the Memphis cotton market, even tried to "pay them out" of it all: make some sort of a deal with the government. But the U.S. government just more or less asked him who he thought he was, to say nothing of who he thought *they* were. And that was the end of the matter. I don't suppose anybody had ever heard of plea bargaining back then.

But then on top of all such shenanigans as that there were the kind of people who, as my mother somewhat delicately put it, "stepped aside," more or less, I inferred, out of "passion," though of course she never used that word: they just got "carried away," she said, by another man or another woman and were just too "weak" to resist—like when you got sick and died because, people said, no matter what your ailment was, you just weren't strong enough to "throw it off."

And that's what I always wondered about an attractive young woman who, when I was in the eighth grade, simply disappeared into thin air one cold winter afternoon, leaving her car parked on the

Obion River bridge on the way to Memphis, with the lights still on
and her fur coat still on the front seat. And there was no end to the
speculation that went on about that around town. Some people
thought she and her husband weren't altogether compatible; but the
main thing probably was that she just couldn't stand living in the
same house with her Baptist mother-in-law, who was the biggest boss
in Creation and always reminded me of a buffalo like the ones in our
geography textbook. But others said it wasn't that at all; she had just
fallen for a very attractive young man who had recently come to
town to be the head embalmer up at the funeral home. (But he hadn't
disappeared as yet.) In any case, it was all an abiding—and a pretty
lurid—mystery, and they never found her body in the river or
anywhere else. The whole town was really divided over it too—and
really sort of *put out* into the bargain—because nobody would ever
know for sure what happened.

(People can take most anything, I've found, if you'll only let
them finally know what really happened behind the scenes. What
they can't stand is being just *left out* of the whole thing.)

And in a town like ours there was always *something*. Why, it
wasn't but a few years ago that I came back from a trip to England
one summer (I'm an English teacher and tell all my friends over there
that I have a vested interest in their country) and all my colleagues
asked me if I wasn't from Woodville, Tennessee. And when I said
yes, they proceeded to give me a colorful account of the unexplained
disappearance of the Methodist preacher down there. And funnily
enough, he seemed to have disappeared somewhere in the neighborhood of the Obion River bridge too. And you might say, everybody
thought that was just too much of a good thing because that bridge
and the river itself, for that matter, just weren't that glamorous or
alluring unless they had charms that nobody knew anything about.
But then maybe it was really true what people always said about truth
being stranger than fiction. At least that was one thing about those
two bankers that "went to the bad." You had the satisfaction of
knowing where they were even if you never did find out exactly *why*.

But there was one important difference in the case of the Methodist preacher: he did finally turn up—in Dallas, of all places, in a J.C. Penney store, with no excuse or anything else to offer for himself. Indeed, he said he couldn't even figure out why he was in Dallas itself, much less that particular store: he never had bought anything at any of their stores before. (Of course some people just said, well, they had always known he didn't have any taste to amount to anything: so they had known better from the beginning than to expect him to resurface in Neiman-Marcus.)

Anyhow, this was the strangest Woodville mystery of all because he did duly come back from his Texas exile, but it was something of an anti-climax too because you never did know for sure *what* had actually happened, even if you saw the people involved again. (Amnesia—loss of memory—was what the preacher said was wrong with him. But then some people thought that was just because he couldn't think of anything else, and they added somewhat unkindly that you surely couldn't have lost what you had never had.) But anyhow he even started preaching again, like he, at any rate, was prepared to let bygones be bygones. But a good many members of the congregation weren't prepared to have any of that. And they said they knew *something* was out of kilter about anything so brazen as that and some of them even said they had stopped paying their pledges and would just wait to see how things came out before starting back again. And if it didn't all hurry up and get straightened out before long, they just might ask for their "letters" and move their membership elsewhere.

But that wasn't all: a couple of months later the church itself caught on fire one cold winter night and would have burned down if the town hadn't had a pretty good group of volunteer firemen. And of course arson was suspected, according to the grapevine. But again, how would that sort of thing make the preacher's situation any better? That *was* a mystery. Now of course if it had been his house, everybody could have said he was just trying to burn up his wife, who *was* a pretty tall order and a grammar school principal as well, to say nothing of the children, who mostly took after her. And then, as if this wasn't enough, right in the middle of all this commotion I even heard him preach a funeral (one of our distant cousins, as a matter of fact) on the text of "grasshoppers" (Job 39:20), which still remains a curiosity to me right this minute because I never could understand in what way it might refer to the cousin and his nostrils, to say nothing of the grasshopper himself. ("Canst thou make him afraid as a grasshopper? The glory of his nostrils is terrible.")

Well, nobody ever did know for sure what it was all about; but most people said, never mind, there was always a *method* in people's madness and sooner or later murder *would* out. But so far as I know it never has. (My aunt—the one who had those twenty first cousins right on the scene—said, well, what did it matter because in any case his wife was *ten times smarter* than he was? But when I ventured to reply that maybe that was the source of the trouble, it was not well received.)

At one point, I believe, the preacher did say the reason he made for the bridge for his "disappearance" was a rumor that reached him to the effect that there was a drug racket being carried on from back in the woods which bordered on the bridge and he wanted to find out more about it and then tell the law so it could all be put a stop to without unfortunate publicity for the town. (As if we hadn't already had quite enough.) But I'm happy to say that this was all just too far-fetched for most people to believe. Even lying has to be fairly credible, you know.

Finally, as most people said you might have expected, he and his wife separated; and he left the ministry and moved out to Texas and remarried (more than once, I think). And his wife went back to school to study for her Master's degree in "human behavior," as if she hadn't already had a crash course in that subject in her own household. But it all remained one of the unsolved mysteries of the town and maybe the most bizarre of them all. After all, though these tales had all had their own share of "mystery" and none of them was ever completely "solved," this was the only one that had ever involved grasshoppers. But then, according to my father, what else could you expect? Like he had always said: no matter what, you just couldn't ever beat *folks*.

The Last Old Maid in Town

When I was growing up, I used to be ashamed of my parents' ages: my mother was forty when I was born and my father, forty-five. Strangely enough, I didn't realize they were older than the parents of my contemporaries until I was well on into grammar school. I do remember one time that a friend of my father's, whom I didn't particularly like, was teasing me about my great affection for him: I had boasted that my father could do *anything*. And the man, who must have been about my father's age himself, said, "Why, boy, there're a lot of things your father can't do simply because he's getting old. Why, he's fifty, I'll bet, right now." I was stunned, I remember, and tried to put it all out of my head: my father couldn't be that old. I thought. The next thing I knew, he would be dead. And that was too awful to contemplate.

I suppose I could have done some simple adding and subtracting, but I didn't. (Was I afraid of what I might find out?) But I did know that Pa, my father's father and the only one of my grandparents I ever knew, was a Confederate veteran, And that must have meant something, but I didn't want to think about it. One of my playmates had recently lost her mother, and I was terrified that one or both of my parents might die or be killed in an automobile wreck or some-thing—just like in the newspaper headlines.

But these were all things I didn't like to dwell on—my parents' ages, their own mortality—any more than I might have liked then to contemplate my own death. So for a number of years I just rocked along, burying my head in the sand and not *thinking* about any of it. But finally revelation had to come, I suppose; and it came in a rather bizarre way. We were then on the verge of World War II, and every-body had to sign up for ration books—at least all adults, as I recall. And shortly after my parents had gotten their books, I found them lying somewhere about the house and, out of nothing but idle curiosity, took a look at them. And there were the facts, signed, sealed, and very official. My father was listed as being fifty-five and my mother as fifty. I was ten myself, and I was horrified. So they really were all that much older! I really was the child of *old* people who probably didn't have many years left to them, and all my fears of being orphaned and bereft weren't completely idle. From that moment, I began to feel a something about my own self that might be peculiar or atypical, something that set me apart from my contemporaries.

Before me there yawned vast abysms of time, with what horrors I knew not but could only guess. Whatever they might be, I knew there were some things I could count on: seeing my parents get old while I was still very young, seeing them die while I was still a child perhaps—being left alone in the world, not belonging to anybody, not really wanted by anybody. And it was almost too awful to contemplate. What would I do, where would I go, what would become of me? My parents' own families were all as old or older than they were, so there would be no help from that quarter. And hadn't I already detected perhaps a note of amusement in my aunts' and uncles' attitudes toward me—that somehow they regarded me as a freak, an anomaly, an *indulgence* on the part of my parents? Wasn't there something somehow *funny* in my very existence, the only child of older parents who had married "late in life?" ("I'll never forget the day we heard the news of your father's marriage! None of us had known a thing about it—almost like he was trying to hide it from us. Why, I went in the store that morning and asked for him; and your Uncle Buford, who was holding down the fort, said 'Why, he's gone to Memphis on his honeymoon!' You could have knocked me over with a feather!")

Then later there was the surprise, even shock, you might almost say, of my own birth. ("I'll never forget how excited your father was that morning! He called all of us in the family up and told us he had a football player for a son!") This always with a laugh and a knowing aside toward me, the least athletically inclined boy imaginable. (Had

I failed my father somehow?) Another old acquaintance told me, in later years, that they had even feared for my mother's safety during delivery at her time of life, ("Why, we were playing bridge that night, just across the street from your house. And we weren't about to leave until you had put in your appearance: we all knew your mother might have a bad time of it. But do you know, we got so engrossed in our bridge game that the doctor came and went, and you had arrived, and we never knew it!") This always with much laughter—not unkind—after I was grown and able to assess the facts of the case for myself.

But gradually, as I was growing up, I began to take all this information in and assimilate it as best I could—the stories, the tales of my parents' wedding and early married life, my own birth and early childhood. And I suppose, finally, my principal reaction—at least when I was young—was one of shame: shame that I might have been an afterthought in my parents' lives, shame, on the other hand, that they might have wanted me very badly indeed but had not been able to conceive me until eight years after their marriage, above all, shame that I was the product of old people's lusts.

I would have given anything for young and glamorous parents, even perhaps a pair of "swingers," as they might be called today. Not only their clothes and our house (an old L-shaped affair, where you had to walk through rooms to get to other rooms) were tacky, I decided; we didn't even have a real car, just used the truck that belonged to my father and Uncle Buford's supply store. And everywhere we went, we had to go in that—to Memphis or around town, to visit out in the country, no matter where. And everyone could see our shame. Before my time, I think, the store's truck had even been painted in the familiar Purina checkerboard pattern, but I was spared that.

None of this seemed to embarrass them, of course—only me. They cared little, apparently, for appearances. And they loved nothing better than telling jokes on themselves, especially about their marriage and early married life—things which shamed me inexpressibly because I thought of it all as somehow unsuitable for their place and their years. My mother would tell, with great glee, about how my father had always boasted that when he got married, there would be a sign mailed right beside the front door declaring him "boss and manager" of the house. But shortly after they were married, she said, and had moved into their new house (it was really my mother's own childhood home that they had remodeled), an old friend passed by just as my father—to help my mother out—was sweeping off the porch and hollered to him and asked him where his sign was. But my father just smiled and shook his head and never said a word. And he didn't do much more than that when my mother would tell it on him in later years—he was usually so outspoken, even boisterous in his opinion, his likes and dislikes. (Had my mother somehow tamed him? It was somehow shocking to me that either of them might still be capable of such passion.)

Of course, there were jokes at her expense too—ones she didn't mind telling either. And one was about their honeymoon, which they had spent at the Gayoso Hotel in Memphis, which I remember as a once elegant hostelry, now, in my childhood, on the downgrade, with hideous murals of De Soto discovering the Mississippi in its lobby— that same lobby that General Forrest's men had ridden into during a lightning raid on Memphis under Federal occupation. Naturally, the thought of my parents' having a *honeymoon* (like you were always seeing in the movies, like you were always hearing from younger couples) was distasteful to me. Perhaps the sex lives of our parents— or the thought of them—is distasteful to all of us. But again, it all seemed to me that they were too old for such things: they should have known better. My mother, for the first and last time in her life, she said, even wore a silk nightgown, the mention of which always made me blush. And what did they do in Memphis anyway, I always wanted to know. Well, they said they just went to some shows and ball games and that was about it—nothing really exciting and just as staid as they were.

But the funniest thing was what happened to them just as they were leaving home for Memphis, right after their marriage. They had been married up at my mother's aunt's house (her own parents were already dead then); and the ceremony had been a very quiet and simple one, so there had been only some cousins and her aunt and Uncle Buford to "stand up" with them. But it was a gay enough affair for all that, I gather. And afterwards there was a regular concourse of friends to see them off at the station for Memphis on the night train. In those days (1922) of course that was the only way to travel considerable distances—by train; and I suppose the ceremony had been planned accordingly—so they could catch that particular train.

The train duly arrived, and my parents boarded it. But there was still rice dripping from their clothes—from where they had been pelted by their friends and well-wishers at the station. So when the conductor came down the aisle to take their tickets, he observed their situation and remarked, "There seem to be more newlyweds getting on the train at Woodville than any other town on my run." "Tell me," he asked my father, "are there any old maids at all left there now?" And my father looked him mock-seriously in the eye and said, "No, sir, this was the last one left!"

When my mother got to that part of the story—and it was nearly always she who told it, she would burst into laughter and say, "I should have left him right then." And all the listeners would cluck their tongues and smile as though to say, of course, they knew she wouldn't have for anything in the world, and it was all just my father's well-known predisposition for mischief anyhow. But finally, after I had gotten to be a teenager, it got so that tale troubled me—as though somehow they were trying to hang on to the coquettishness of youth though by that time both well stricken in years. I found it tiresome, annoying even to have them still almost *flirting* with each other under my very nose, so to speak. And so once, when I was in the eighth grade, I think, I heard my mother recount the tale once more to some of the cousins. And when she came to the coda after the punch line (my father's) and said, "I should have left him right then," everyone laughed right on schedule except for me. And I spoke up, rather brightly, and said, "Well, if you had, wouldn't I have been in a *mell of a hess*?" And there was more laughter still, whether at my wit or my boldness I never knew. But my mother gave me a look then that I've never forgotten, as though to say she hadn't realized until then that I was almost grown, at any rate old enough to know about "those things" and also as though, for the first time, she might be seeing me as more than a child, perhaps even a potential adult. And for one brief moment there was almost a look of horror in her eyes—something I then didn't understand and am not altogether sure that I do now.

Did she wonder then what she and my father had wrought between them? Did she wonder what I might be thinking of them as adults, not just as parents—what I might have been thinking of their relationship, marital and otherwise, what I might be thinking of their middle age now verging on old age and I only in my teens? I'll never know now, but I've never forgotten the look she gave me—something stricken, I think, and somehow sad. Had I somehow penetrated their private world, their aging romance (and they did still love each other very much, I believe) with my youth, my brashness, my impudence? Had I made her see, if only for a moment, that I thought it all somehow indecorous and unsuitable? Again, I don't know. But I did realize then that I had somehow hurt her in way I didn't altogether understand. And I was sorry.

All the things that I had feared more or less did really happen. Both my parents died while I was still comparatively young, and I was left alone—no brothers or sister, just Uncle Buford, after the older uncles had died, and some first cousins. But by that time I had begun to see something of what my older parents had given me— besides the sense of shame that I used to feel. And it wasn't altogether on one side of the ledger either. Sure, I had a sense of the past, a sense of history from having more or less grown up in the house with it. I knew the county genealogies about as well as anyone else, certainly better than most of my contemporaries. And I knew something—a great deal, I felt—of the tragedies of old age, of living on beyond one's time, of what might be called the *cruelties* of modern medicine. (My father had literally dropped dead one morning at the breakfast table; but it seemed as though, after years of illness, my mother couldn't ever die.) Perhaps I had experienced *King Lear* before my time; at least, I felt, I had experienced it for real. But also I had become something of an oracle myself: I was the one to whom people turned now for verification of dates and facts about the past. And why shouldn't I know, with such a background as my own?

But there were some things on the positive side too, albeit some of them I would not have sought on my own. There was the sense of apartness, the sense of remoteness that came with being the only child of older parents: I had learned to look and, more important, I had learned to listen. (How many times had I been told that children should be seen and not heard?) So I had been listening to old people talk all my life—reminiscing, sorrowing, rejoicing, ruminating—it didn't matter which, really. And I was outside their world—part of it yet not of it, with a foot in past and present. More and more, then, that became my role—that of the observer, above all, the listener. Set apart from my contemporaries because of my origins, I was set apart from my parents and their families because of the great disparity of age. Perhaps I didn't belong anywhere, finally. And yet I've come to see that that was not so either, and it explains a lot of things about me perhaps.

It's why I listen as well as look, why I listen as well as talk. It's why I never in my life have felt particularly intimate with anyone. It's why, all my life, I've felt very much alone—not necessarily lonely, just alone. But I know now that it's why I think the way I do, behave the way I do, why I am the person that I am—different from all others as we all must finally be. And I know now that it's why, more and more, as I get older myself, I realize that my function must be that of the rememberer, the celebrator of the pieties of time and place—the past that I came out of yet was not a part of, the town, the county which own me—and will own me—all the days of my life.

It's finally the reason that I write what I do and as I do—the old times, the old tales, of both sorrow and joy, with the present knowledge and blessing they continually confer. It's finally the reason—I know it now—that I tell all my tales or—if you will—sing all my songs, and especially this one now which I have tried to set down here.

The Girls

My mother belonged to two clubs, equally different and equally important. First, there was the Tuesday Bridge Club, which she had joined before World War I, if you can believe that. Then there was the Review Club, which came along about the time she was married in 1922. And the members of course—as in Helen Hokinson's cartoons in *The New Yorker* of the 1940s and 1950s were uniformly called "the girls," why, I never knew except it was a way of suggesting that they weren't *quite* so old as one thought. On the other hand, I believe it was the bridge club members which seemed to have a deadlock on that nickname. After all, the bridge club was more feisty: they played with what used to be considered "spot" cards too. And some of them actually *smoked*, which my mother thought was mostly an attempt to prolong youth (or the appearance of it) as long as possible. Why else would they light up a cigarette, then after two or three puffs, simply lay it down in the ash tray and not touch it again? And by and large, they didn't inhale either.

The Review Club, her book club, was more sedate and met on the second and fourth Monday nights of every month, excluding June, July, and August. And it had something of a higher moral tone: giving reports on the world's work, reviewing current best-sellers (though what they really wanted was mainly a summary of each volume), anything that led to that strange commodity known as "culture." There were four or five book clubs in Woodville when I was growing up, organized mainly along the lines of age. The oldest—and I'm sure they thought the most elite—was called the Wednesday Book Club but as a rule simply *The* Book Club; and it was composed mainly of dowagers, mostly from the "older" families. Then the Review Club, the only one which met at night because, I was told, some of them were teachers and others "businesswomen" and afternoon socializing was not something they could take on. The rest of the book clubs, though, followed the lead of *The* Book Club and met on Wednesday afternoon, which was often called "Book Club Day."

The third of these exercises in culture was called the Junior Book Club, and it was composed mainly of the daughters of the senior group. It was tacitly understood that in due course these younger women, these "daughters" would themselves become *The* Book Club when the seniors had mostly passed on to their reward, which of course seemed appropriate, preserving the legitimacy of the succession.

So they were different groups and served different needs and different kinds of women. Whereas the Tuesday Bridge Club assumed a more social function—three-course luncheons with *hats*—the Review Club (though it thrived on apricot ice cream whose dasher I got to lick) was more sedate and even undertook good works from time to time. And it might have been considered more "proper" than the other: you didn't hear the gossip in that group that you got in the bridge club, some of it even from time to time approaching the "indelicate." And I think it was there that most of their "news" was circulated—mostly "girl talk"—but nonetheless savory for all that.

But for pomp and circumstance none of these organizations could hold a candle to *The* Book Club. First of all, you had to *apply* to get in; it wasn't ever "by invitation." And if you had a guest from out of town, she might be invited to a meeting of the club but you couldn't be if you weren't a member yourself. Preachers' wives were always invited as "honorary members." And new brides were invited *once* but never again unless they eventually became members themselves. Was this all an attempt to preserve a high social tone for a small town organization, making both applicants and members bend the knee at suitable times—just to show where they *stood*? I couldn't imagine that these curious practices could serve any other purpose. I thought the bridge club served another end too—not "culture" but perhaps "fun" and "style." And I couldn't see them serving loftier ends, though they might have remained faithful to more elegant ones. The one "serious" end they did observe took place during the church revivals in the summer, when, as they said, they always "gave way," it was tacitly understood, for dignity's sake. O and yes, they too invited the preachers' wives (as a rule only Methodist, Baptist, and Presbyterian—other denominations didn't count) but only as "tea guests," because it was always understood that such ladies didn't play cards.

Of course it all sounds ridiculous now, but nothing could be more so than, say, the DAR, who in 1939 forbade Marian Anderson's singing in their auditorium in Washington, thus galvanizing Eleanor Roosevelt into getting one of her husband's cabinet members into opening the Lincoln Memorial free to all comers that Easter afternoon. And besides, I always thought that high and mighty organization was a sort of contradiction against itself. Yes, they were exclusive all right: you had to be qualified by a Revolutionary blood line to apply for membership, *but* not all the members were necessarily in the upper echelons of what passed for society, which could constitute something of an embarrassment. I never knew how they solved that dilemma. But perhaps it was something like FDR's strategy of the put-down he used in addressing the Daughters about that time. I'm not certain exactly what the occasion was, but he began with "Fellow immigrants. . . . "

Every Friday Afternoon

I don't know that any of us were ever sure just why we went out to Nutbush every Friday afternoon, but always we went in my car because I was the only one in the group who had one. Of course it was our senior year in high school too, and I guess we thought we could kick up our heels then and take some liberties, being that our teen years were almost over and we would soon be entering the "real" world. But then why did we go out to Nutbush—the little wide place in the road with the weird name that more or less straddled the line between our own county and the one to its immediate east? That was never clear either.

Perhaps it all had something to do with just that fact—it was to the east of us, not the west, where all you could do was drive down the bluff, not then completely smothered in kudzu vines, past Cypress Lake, which was an "arm" of the river (the Mississippi naturally—there was no other for any of us, just like *the War*) and where many folks in town had their "vacation" houses. And nearly all of them were naturally built on stilts because of the high water—nobody much said "flood" (did that sound too cataclysmic?)—which periodically backed up out of the *cul de sac* where most of the houses were. And then after driving past what seemed as many miles as you could imagine you ran headlong into the climax of your excursion— the first glimpse of the river, with Arkansas looming far away on the other side. But we had been doing that all our lives and really couldn't imagine going anywhere else for our sights and scenery, no matter how grand.

But Nutbush was not scenery. Part of what gave it its fascination was that it was pointing in another direction, another time, looking toward Nashville and Knoxville, the Smokies (which we were told were older and "smoother" than the Rockies out west) and finally the

Atlantic itself, the very name of which sounded ancient and grand but also menacing too, unlike the Pacific, which suggested the peace and quiet of twilight and the setting sun. But all that was foreign to us—*beaches* and *ships*, even *seafood* and, ultimately, the concept of "abroad," as most people called it. Of course hardly any of us in those days had ever tasted real seafood. For most of us, all we knew of such things was just fried catfish—the only thing we had tasted out of the water, fresh or salt—and, along with watermelon, considered quintessentially southern, though I detested them both (but of course felt guilty for doing so). But whatever the case, I believe we all thought, with our growing up, almost on the edge of adulthood now, we deserved something like the new horizon, the different direction which was Nutbush.

We hadn't ever looked at any of it that way before. Yes, the river was grand but, despite its age, with something of the present and future too, the West still out there, waiting to be fully discovered and the river our highway to the unknown, the wonders of Memphis and New Orleans, and if we looked the other way, even St. Louis and ultimately, Cincinnati and Pittsburgh. But Nutbush was also new and somewhat unknown to us too. And I believe we all somehow identified it with morning, the rising sun, though its own past was more than ancient. (People always spoke of the Old World when looking that way, to the east.) It was also on a kind of border, as I said: right between the two counties, right between the old and the new, as people often said of our country itself. And thus we had something of both past and future, some kind of continuity that helped to identify our whereabouts and fix our place until we knew them as part of our very selves, our own world and time.

$$* * *$$

There were usually five or six of us—Ann Louise Parker, then Martha Alice Craig and Mary Jane Estes and two or three boys besides me, to even up things—often Floyd Martin and Tom Lucas, if we could get them all together. But like I said, I was the only one who had a car: until then my folks simply drove wherever they had to go in the pickup truck that belonged to my father and uncle's hardware store. But now we were forced to go on to higher things since I was old enough to have dates and be ashamed of the antiquated conveyance I would be forced to use—or at least I felt so, whatever my parents thought. Their main priority then and always was saving money for what, as a small boy, I call my "keduation." And in due course my father saw me through from the first grade on to the Ph.D. at Yale—perhaps the proudest achievement in his life, and rightly so for somebody who had never been to high school.

So every Friday afternoon, when school let out, we felt we had this freedom coming to us, we deserved it; and we thought it was high time to kick up our heels and feel our oats. It was hard on Floyd and Tom since they were more or less on the football team, but that was mostly just as substitutes. But somehow they always found a way of sneaking out early, especially if it looked as though there would be no immediate call for their services. And besides, they could always sneak back in before it got too late for the game, before they had really been missed. And anyway, they weren't star performers and their being absent wasn't going to make or break things that night.

The girls were somewhat different: their presence or absence didn't seem to really matter, as long as they *behaved*—not too much giggling and teasing and of course nothing off-color from either them or us. But sometimes that was a tall order, especially for somebody like Ann Louise, who was always the ring leader in whatever foolishness was going to take place, and of course Martha Alice was more or less her boon companion (they were some kind of cousins was the reason why, I think). And whatever other girls were around were something like their hangers-on—supporting players like in the movies, you might say.

But anyhow every Friday it all began with a trip to Archie Long's drugstore down on the square—as soon as the final bell rang and we were turned loose. And before I could even get there myself there would be a regular pile of folks all jammed in my car, ready to go down to Archie's for an ice-cream cone, then, after a stop at the hardware store (which dealt in other things too—"staple" groceries, for one) to see whether my father had gotten in any Hershey bars, a scarce item in those years right after World War II, it was finally on to Mary Jane's grandmother's (the local hotel, which was called the Estes House) for some of that lady's specialty, homemade dill pickle. And it was only about then we knew we were safe and, one way or another, had managed to shed all the extra added attractions or, as my father called them, the boosters so now just our "inner circle" was left and we could make for the rural regions—usually, Nutbush, to enjoy our own company and no one else's.

Why this peculiar diet, which was always part of our Friday ritual, didn't make for a whole epidemic of gastric upheavals I'll never know; perhaps we were saved by the resilience of our youth and whatever else went with it. But somehow we all managed to survive and went right on with the world and time, taking no thought for the morrow and whatever the future might bring. Surely, we all thought, it didn't have anything to say to us. All we had to do with ourselves and with the world right then was simply continuing to grow up, driving on eastward, away from the fall afternoon and the sinking sun, maybe even the river, sometimes hollering out the window at friends, not so fortunate as we were, who were plodding on their way homeward, perhaps with chores awaiting them there, certainly not so much leisure as we, in our modest good fortune, could expect. God knew what they thought of us, I suspect; but I'm sure we didn't mind seeming somewhat "chosen" for the moment, perhaps even a little envied.

But then what did we do with ourselves when we got to Nutbush? What was there to see, what was there to do? Well, not much really—look at the Methodist and Baptist Churches, even the Cumberland Presbyterian one (somewhat wasting away now because I had heard someone say that breed was dying off), go see the old cemetery with its full quota of Confederate graves on display, some-times even a Stars and Bars firmly planted in the grass above them, and recalling to ourselves that there was still a Confederate Memorial Day to be remembered along with the "Yankee" one. And then there were the two cotton gins, going hot and heavy in the fall weather and the crop was coming on strong and the July flies were making their own shrill music in the increasing twilight.

It was a drowsy, even sleepy time, with not yet a nip of fall in the air, but still "fallified," as my mother used to say, with a kind of glare in the afternoon sun. But we went on with our own concerns, our own version of gossip—tales about who was dating whom or who wanted to date whom, what the coming winter, then spring might be sending us—also what colleges we might be headed for, if we were fortunate enough, a year from now and what we wanted to do with ourselves in later life—all those old and quiet things the young imagine so freely yet knowing so little of what really lies ahead.

Sex? Well, no because right now we were neither boys nor girls but just friends, with no fish to fry or hearts to break. There was too much going on, too much to look forward to at the moment. Yes, of course we knew about the ritual and the practice of it all; but that could wait till some future time. We were in no hurry. And in spite of everything, perhaps right then we didn't care. Youth is not always up and at 'em; sometimes it wants only to watch and wait.

There were a few more wonders, a few more sights, almost rituals for us now, to check in with before we headed back home— Miss Walker's chrysanthemum beds, for one thing, always proudly billed (in our local weekly paper) as something to display right now in the autumn when all else seemed hastening on its way to disso-lution, with the star of the show being the "Miss Edna" chrysan-themum she was supposed to have developed and named of course for herself. (I suppose she had the first nursery ever in captivity in our world.) And if we were lucky, we might even catch a glimpse of the old girl herself working among her flowers, and that was always diverting because she was the only woman we had ever seen wearing men's pants for such undertakings. The diamond earrings she must have been born with she never took off, apparently: nobody had ever seen her without them.

And she had some other characteristics that we all knew about too—for one thing, a very sharp tongue. There was one old man down the road from her that used to tease her off and on about her state of single blessedness—why had she never married, he wanted to know. But she always gave him as good as he sent: she just replied that she must not have been as anxious to get married as his wife had been.

She was also a staunch member of the Church of Christ, which didn't hold with instrumental music in church: they just hauled off and "heisted" a tune under their own steam, with Miss Edna as their leader. But every now and then she would disappear out the side door, where she always sat, only to return a moment or two later looking somewhat more at ease; and everybody knew she had just gone out to spit, leading the singing put such a strain on her voice. (A few irreverent spirits suggested that she had been dipping snuff, but nobody really believed that for a minute.) One of her characteristic selections for getting the service off to a good start was the old hymn known to almost everybody as "Revive Us Again!" And its chorus always concluded with "Hallelujah, Thine the glory; Hallelujah, Amen! / Hallelujah, Thine the glory; Revive us again!" And when she put her whole heart and mind behind that one, you knew the Lord was listening—or at any rate, had better be, because it wasn't just a *request*; it was a *demand*.

And finally there were always Mr. Olin Dorsey's prize bulls to look at too as we drove by his dairy farm—the ones he kept for "breeding" purposes, though, at our age, we were still somewhat hazy in our knowledge of just how and why and what all such things meant, especially the "breeding schedule" and why anybody needed one for *that*. But we had to give them all a look-see, check them off for another week: that was what Nutbush (unlike the river and its perpetual rolling along?) *meant*, what you took for granted, what you understood in a world which, at least for you, seemed never destined to change. And finally of course there were things of which we could not possibly have dreamed then, not even looming on the horizon yet but waiting for us in the future—with people and places and thoughts even harder to imagine: Elvis himself growing up right that minute in the shotgun house down in Tupelo and Tina Turner perhaps walking down the road right there in Nutbush already singing to herself.

Auntee and the Two Nieces

Auntee, who was not really my aunt but a very dear cousin of my mother's, had two nieces, Mary Sue and Frances, who always called her that. And since they were in many ways the center of her life and I loved her dearly also, I followed their lead and called her Auntee too. (Her given name was really Ada, but she had always despised it.) Anyway, she had married an old widower and raised his two children by a previous marriage (to a foot-washing Baptist, by the way); but she never had any children of her own. And perhaps it was just as well because for thirty years she was more or less having to nurse and ultimately bury *somebody*—first, her husband and then the two old-maid cousins, "the Moss girls," as my mother called them, who had been something like foster parents to her after her own mother had died when she was two. But the two nieces were *hers*, and she could love them and chasten them and anything else that had to be done to keep them in line.

And they were both of them very much like her—but different sides of her, I thought. Mary Sue was rambunctious and plainspoken and quick to talk back to anybody that tried to tell her what to do; so in due course she had naturally up and married a man whose family owned a lot of land down in the Mississippi Bottom and all talked entirely too much about money (they were always wondering how much somebody was "worth"), to say nothing of having a mother who had a gold tooth. Not really "our" kind of folks, the Moss girls always said. But Frances married a young doctor, whose folks were more genteel—some of them doctors too—and she had a softer tongue than Mary Sue; but she was just as well able to stand up for herself too when the time came. And in matters of principle they were both Auntee's own nieces; you could tell that right away. Some things you just you didn't *do*: you didn't ever lie or go back on your word, and you certainly didn't tell everything you knew, about your business or your family or anything else, and especially your husband, even if he wasn't any better than he ought to be.

Because that seemed like the Achilles' heel for them both. Mary Sue, after twenty years of matrimony and four children, finally decided that she had heard quite enough about big landowners and gold teeth, to say nothing of her husband, who was named Troy, tomcatting around all over the county. And Frances finally had to leave her husband, who had started off with a good medical practice, take her two daughters (both of them pretty), and go back home to live with her parents, while keeping books at the Ford agency. And as far as I know, her husband hadn't been up to anything on the side either; just got too fond of Jack Daniel's, I think. But that wasn't putting food on the table. Later on, after he had gotten himself "straightened out," as the family always put it, he married again and had another daughter.

But Frances never remarried: I think she had just had enough of the whole thing, marriage and all that went with it. (She told somebody she just wanted to get off the roller coaster and be quiet for a while.) But Mary Sue went them all one better because after she and Troy were divorced, he married again—twice; but after a good many years of *that* (the first one left him, and the other one died) he seemed to have had enough excitement and of course Mary Sue had never really gotten over him either. So, what with some encouragement from the children and even a certain amount of inclination of their own, they got back together and married again, and it looked like everybody was satisfied with the way it had all turned out.

But to get back to the differences between the two of them, I always thought Mary Sue was more like the colorful, "public" side of Auntee and Frances was the gentler, more "well-behaved"—the side that was more "private" and discreet. But both sides were part of the same personality: there was nothing "split" about them or Auntee either. And why should there have been, I always thought. You can speak softly or sharply either one, depending on the provocation, and I never understood why that seemed such a mystery to many people. On the one hand, Mary Sue, who taught school before she married, could say what she really thought about the drones and bureaucrats who, more and more, populated the teaching profession. ("They want to have a nose in everybody's business in the world and 'supervise' everything you do and then some, and everything they have anything to do with has got to be in constant use, it's got to *work*. To tell the truth, if they had their way, they'd like to have somebody sitting on every commode in every rest room on the premises every minute of the day—and furthermore, they'd want to know what you're wiping with too.")

And usually the conversation stopped right there, as it did when Auntee was complaining to whoever *she* was talking to (it didn't matter) about her friend poor Miss Sally Conroy's folks being unable to get "decent" help to look after her in her old age. ("That woman they've got up there with her now is just not of the right calibre, what with men calling her up in the middle of the night and all kinds of cute things going on.") But if her listener ventured to remind her that in these days sometimes it wasn't what you *wanted* but what you could *get* in such matters, she would explode with, "O the Devil, I've had lots of tough luck in my life, but I've never yet had a wench in my house!" And of course she knew that you had to choose your audience for that kind of freedom of speech, but I think she believed it didn't hurt to expose some kinds of folks to "reality" now and then.

Naturally, it was Auntee (who else?) that explained the double standard of sexual morality to me when I was growing up and my juvenile sense of justice was violated when the women in the magazines my mother took always paid and paid for their "misbehavior" but the men got off scot-free. But she rose to the occasion handsomely enough by pulling down her corset as though girding for battle, and saying, like she was the pope making a pronouncement on faith and morals, "Well, you see, Baby, men are *weak*. And if it weren't for women upholding the moral standards of the community, we just wouldn't have any!" And then she added, like an afterthought or a *coda* in a piece of music, "because the world's going to Hell fast enough as it is." And that settled that. And in due course I heard Mary Sue say something pretty much like the same thing, especially after she had had *her* husband trouble. ("There's not a man in the world you can really trust below the belt.")

But you never would have heard Frances say anything like that at all. When she had her own marital trouble, I don't think she got as mad about it all as Mary Sue; at any rate, she didn't talk about it so much. She simply faced facts and acted promptly, just talking (discreetly) to her husband's brother, who was also a doctor, and, with his approval, had her husband quietly committed to the state psychiatric hospital in Memphis. And then she told his family and her own that she hoped they could help him because *she* couldn't worry about him any more now: she had her living to make and two daughters to raise.

And that was like Auntee also: *she* never cried over spilled milk and the world was as it was and you couldn't worry about anything else but your share of it. Just like when her husband was in Memphis in the hospital with his last illness under the care of the great Dr. Livermore (yes, that was really his name), and he just up and told her, straight out, that her husband was going to *die* (nothing like "pass away" for *him*) and she might as well face facts and get ready to go on with her own life without him, which in due course she certainly did. And for the rest of her life, whenever Dr. Livermore's name was mentioned, she would nod wisely and say, "That man taught me how to *live!*" And that was more like Frances.

I always had a feeling that Mary Sue, as the first grandchild in Auntee's family, got more attention than Frances—partly because she asked for it. The squeaking wheel does usually get the oil. And sometimes you would have thought she was the only woman in captivity who had had husband trouble. But Troy did provide for her (with a good settlement, I believe) when he left her, but not until after he had told her, "You know, you're a good woman, but there's just no market for good women!" And Mary Sue died laughing, which is exactly what Auntee would have done and pretty much like the line she took when she heard that her own husband's "wild" younger brother had been shot dead in a crap game on the Fourth of July not long after she was married. But she said her main job was looking after his brother, and she couldn't waste any time worrying over *him*: she was just glad the son of a bitch was dead.

One thing I ought to say now just to set the record straight. Though the old-maid cousins were very straitlaced about people's morals—and especially women's (the double standard again?), they could always make allowances for men—and especially one that was always in and out of trouble but nevertheless always made them laugh—the kind they would call "that rascal." And I think, as strange as it may seem, Auntee got part of that "side" of herself from them. I know they often called her "Charley Moss," after my mother's brother, who was something of a rounder and, I'm sure, one of the few people in the world who ever ventured to mention anything remotely off-color to them—like the time he observed that one of his wife's rather grand relations didn't marry until late in life because she hated to leave one of her cousins, another spinster with whom she had shared her "old colonial home" for so many years. But she finally gave in and married the cousin's brother so then they could all live together. And not only that, he said: the new sister-in-law even went on their honeymoon with them so he could sleep with one of them one night and the other one the next. And the Moss girls giggled up a storm, all the while telling Uncle Charley he ought to be ashamed of himself.

Well, the years went along and the Moss girls finally went on to their reward; but they were still very much alive in Auntee's and everybody else's memory. I well remember what she said when an in-law connection of theirs, who had been living with a black woman for a good many years (he always called her his "cook"), himself gave up the ghost, naturally in the midst of a good deal of talk and speculation around town. (The woman even sat on the front row with the family at the funeral too, but Auntee said there was no use getting on a high horse about *that*: that was exactly where she *belonged*.) But of course just *mentioning* her would have been outrageous enough, as far as the Moss girls were concerned. And when I made bold to ask Auntee what she herself thought about it, morally or otherwise, and what she reckoned the "girls" would say, it didn't faze her one iota. She said she really couldn't say what the Almighty might think about it all because it was naturally His business and not any of ours, but she was pretty sure that when the two "girls" got the news, they opened an eye or two down there at Cedar Grove Cemetery where all our folks were buried.

But, you know, when it's all said and done, you never really know what people are going to do—or even what they're thinking. Because when Auntee herself died some years later, her will (and she had inherited—deservedly—everything the "girls" had) revealed that she wanted it all to go to Mary Sue—nothing to Frances or anybody else. And of course that was strictly her own business and nobody else's. But I still wondered why she didn't leave something to Frances—maybe one of the two beautiful diamond rings her husband had given her when they married, before he had lost most of his money in the Depression. But then I thought, well, Mary Sue was the one who had complained the most about her lot in life, while Frances had said little—just went on with her own business, raising two fine daughters, very popular in her hometown, even being elected to public office there for several terms.

I did hear her say one time that she was right tired of hearing Auntee always referring to Mary Sue as "poor Mary Sue." Frances didn't seem to think she needed all that much sympathy; after all, she had been well provided for when Troy left her and he had even come back to her in due course. So what was so pitiful about that? She herself, she said, had been left high and dry by the husband who had seemed to have such a promising future before him and then had had to go to work to make a living for both herself and her daughters.

But then, after Auntee died, she told me she just couldn't worry about any of it then or later on: she had more things to do than brood about it all for the rest of her life and, if Mary Sue could stand it, then she reckoned she could too. And when I thought about it that way, I thought, well, yes, that's probably the way Auntee would have looked at it herself.

Graduation from the Air

They were never old fogies, I thought; on the other hand, they were not necessarily the first by whom the new are tried. Middle-of-the-roaders, most of them, I suppose, all except Aunt Gladys, who always wanted to be the first and perhaps the most conspicuous no matter what was in the offing. And she was always eager to keep up with the Joneses. (But then she was an in-law and so in a way didn't count.)

They were all of them people of strong opinions too and naturally great argufiers. But they weren't *contentious* and so weren't really rude; but it didn't take much to set them going, whether the matter was far off or nearer home. And this time the field of conflict was even more remote than usual because it all had its origin in a matter that didn't directly involve any of them—conflicting views about flying. None of them had of course ever flown in an airplane (this back before World War II) and indeed intimated that they could live the rest of their lives without doing so. But Aunt Clara, who was a "real" aunt and not an outsider, made it plain (which was always her way) by saying that she didn't ever want to be a passenger on *anything* where she couldn't tell them to stop and let her off any time she wanted. The rest of them more or less were in a lower key and said that cars and trains and buses could take them anywhere they wanted to go fast enough, certainly if they were behaving themselves.

But not Aunt Gladys, who was married to my father's brother, Uncle John, a high school principal, who she said was a stickler for formality and anything else that was "usual and customary," as the medical profession now calls it, and anyhow was a *lot* older than she was and therefore as slow as Christmas. And she had been having to adjust her life—and her speed—to his as long as they had been married. And on top of that he more or less lived in the past and talked about the old times and the "good old days" as if they were all sanctified, with no virtue existing anywhere else—certainly not in the here and now. (If you taught school long enough, he said, you were bound to come to that conclusion.) And the various school *curricula*, which word he always pronounced as though it was sacred, had all long since started going downhill, with hardly any Latin and history being taught, to say nothing of modern languages and all else that might lift the moral tone of both the individual and the community. And of course it was useless to try reasoning with him: his mind on some subjects had been made up and solidified back around the turn of the century. And that was that.

But of course, that didn't stop Aunt Gladys, who had been wanting to "go up" ever since the Wright brothers had had their fling at Kitty Hawk, to say nothing of Lindbergh's transatlantic adventure. In fact, she had had a second cousin, Mary Charlotte McIntosh, who was out at Le Bourget Airport to see him land. A well-to-do great-aunt, for whom she was named, had taken *her* on a European tour and said she didn't want her to miss anything, which of course (for Aunt Gladys) was pouring salt in the wound; and if it was a choice between Lindbergh and the Eiffel Tower, there was simply no question about what Mary Charlotte preferred. (She'd certainly already seen enough towers and steeples in Europe to last her a good spell.) And the great-aunt said they might as well do it right then, so a French lady had come to their hotel the day before, to teach them both the rudiments of the French language. (I suppose that now we would call it a "crash" course, though some people might object to the sinister implications of the word "crash" in such a context.) Needless to say, every time Mary Charlotte launched into an account of her trip afterwards, which was not seldom, Aunt Gladys would always get up and stomp out to the kitchen or the bathroom (at least one of the necessities, which no one could question) when she got close to the Lindbergh episode.

This of course had all happened a good many years ago, but Aunt Gladys was still trying to keep up with the new and the fashionable.

Of course she naturally embraced the movies in a bear hug when they first appeared. Furthermore, on the side, she taught what they used to call "elocution" but now went by the name of "expression" to grammar school students, which was no trouble at all since the "dramatic" just came naturally to her, she said. So there was no reason why she shouldn't be on board when Hollywood roared through our town, even if it was at first all "silent."

I think my mother believed Aunt Gladys just naturally loved whatever called attention to itself, and the more noise the better. But she had to wait for the sound movies a number of years. Meanwhile she had been one of the first people in town to go all the way to Memphis to see *The Birth of a Nation* and afterwards urged all her friends, family, and anybody else to go take it in as soon as they could: it was really not about the War so much as what the title itself proclaimed—how and why our country as we knew it now had not really come into being until after the War was over and why it would always remain the sort of place it was, one and indivisible forever. And so it was just full of education for all of us, every bit of it based on real history too, despite all that the Yankees were saying. And Lillian Gish was just about the sweetest, prettiest thing you ever saw. No wonder all the male characters wanted to eat her up.

My father of course said that was all he needed to know to keep him away from the whole business—if it intimated that it took the joint efforts of Lincoln, Sherman, and Grant four years just to get this country started to wherever it had ended up. But then since it looked as though the country *was* going to hell before long anyway, what with bootleggers and suffragettes all over the place and all the Negroes just wild to leave and go live in Detroit or somewhere else up there where they could associate—and God knew what else—with white people, maybe it was their handiwork after all. And he was disappointed in the Negroes because he thought they had more sense; but then he never had seen a Yankee yet who had much sense about anything but money: they certainly weren't smart about *folks*.

Some of them, he concluded, even refused to believe in Original Sin and said, on the other hand, maybe there really was such a thing as the perfectibility of man. It was all the work of Clarence Darrow and H. L. Mencken and the Abolitionists, and he didn't give a damn what they thought about evolution. You didn't even need to believe we were descended from apes, for that matter: just look in the mirror any time you wanted and that would *prove* that something awful had happened to all of us way back yonder—and we hadn't been the same since. And, finally, just not to ever get him started on the subject.

Well, that was more or less Aunt Gladys—and perhaps my father—in a nutshell. I think they were born to antagonize each other—Aunt Gladys always ready to go, to see the sights, and often on credit (preferably somebody else's), but my father quite happy to remain sitting on the front porch of the same house we had lived in forever. Really, his wants were few; and though in comfortable circumstances, he never really liked to spend money either unless it was absolutely necessary, and one time he even told me there was nothing he really wanted and, to tell the truth, there was nothing in this world worth buying! Naturally, he never particularly wanted to *go* anywhere. O, he went to Memphis about once a year, and many years ago had actually gone to New York to a hardware convention (he owned a hardware store), and he said he had seen enough to last him the rest of his life. Really, the more he traveled the more it occurred to him that most people were all pretty much alike, so what was the value of that? He already knew that before he left home. And he liked the tried and true, whereas people like "Miss Gladys" (as custom forced him to call her) weren't happy unless they could go somewhere else and see all the sights, mostly the newfangled things that always proclaimed they had come to save the world or mankind from blood, sweat, and tears or something else you had to be a fool to believe.

But anyhow Aunt Gladys was determined that somehow, somewhere she was going to "go up" in an airplane. I'm not even sure she wanted to go to any *place* in particular, but she did want to say she had been "up." At least she could have a modicum of satisfaction at Mary Charlotte McIntosh's expense, she who had seen Lindbergh and his plane arrive so dramatically in Paris but made no bones about being scared to death of flying herself. At least Aunt Gladys wanted to say she had had *that* in her life, and she certainly wasn't afraid either.

But now that we were right on the verge of World War II, her only son, John Jr., was in the air force and was soon learning to fly all over the place. And surely he could do something about it. He had just graduated from college before he got drafted, and she had not yet gotten over the splendor of that ceremony. True, when the time came, the second lieutenants wouldn't wear academic gowns but uniforms; but the sight was just as impressive, like any other ceremony, only this one involved not just the acquisition of more knowledge but expertise also in defending their country. And they were now unquestionably about to become *heroes*, to whom we were all going to be indebted. And so Aunt Gladys was now going to have something she could really talk about and even show you too. And nobody could doubt it.

So she and Uncle John, the high-school principal, drove down to some place on the Gulf Coast, where the air base was located, for the ceremony. Only last year, they had been up to Knoxville to watch John Jr. graduate from the university, and they declared when they returned home it was about the most impressive thing they had ever seen. Like I said, John Jr. was their only child and, to give her credit, Aunt Gladys—and Uncle John too—had every right to be proud of him—bright, good-looking, and always full of fun, and a great tease. And he had already assured them that the ceremony and all the festivities attendant thereupon would mark a great occasion and he would see to it that they had a really good time. And so they were excited as can be—Aunt Gladys more than Uncle John, I'm sure. But then I'm sure that he viewed the whole thing as just another form of

high-school graduation and he had already been there, done that, as
you might say, many times.

But I'm sure neither he nor any of the rest of them could have
foreseen what the harvest would be now. Because no sooner had the
new second lieutenants been given their "bars" which signified their
new rank and then passed with their families down the receiving line,
where the Commander and all his colleagues were prepared to shake
hands with them over the punch bowl, than John Jr. whispered to
them both that he was now going to sneak them aboard one of the
planes parked out on the field and take them up for a little spin. It
must be kept as secret as possible, he added, though it wasn't illegal,
just a little daring, especially at that time when there were so many
outsiders and visitors on the base, to say nothing of all the newspaper
men. And they must come along now but make their exit as incon-
spicuous as possible.

Of course Aunt Gladys was in hog heaven and already planning
the scene she would put together when she met Mary Charlotte
McIntosh again and confronted her with the fact that *she* had also
been "up" and it was as smooth as silk and unquestionably safe
(nothing to be afraid of at all) and would undoubtedly be the transportation of the future. And she was glad that she could say she was
one of its pioneers—and all due to her own son's ability and enterprise. And that would be that.

So of course the first thing they did after they got airborne, all
seat-belted in and ears popping with what sounded like distant gun-
fire, though of course it was probably the increasing altitude, was
drop down to see the sights of the adjacent community, a town of
some 5,000 people. But by now it was getting toward twilight and
John Jr. thought it would be fun to go down and "buzz" the drive-in
movie, at the time a new development in the entertainment industry.
And he told them the movie currently playing there was in Techni-
color and would certainly be a sight to see. And indeed it was
because it was nothing less than *Gone With the Wind*, now released
for the second or third time, and the scene which presented itself to

them like nothing they had ever witnessed before, certainly not diving from such an angle at what seemed more than 100 miles an hour. Because it was obviously the remnants of the Confederate Army left to defend Atlanta, laid out shoulder to shoulder at the railroad station, most of them dead or dying, moaning and groaning as Scarlett frantically searched for Dr. Meade to come deliver Melanie's baby, with exploding shells punctuating the background music, which was "Dixie" played in a minor key.

And I never knew what exactly turned the trick—maybe just what my mother called "too much ice cream." But as soon as they got what looked like less than 100 feet above the ground and, as far as Aunt Gladys was concerned, just on the verge of death, she gave a loud scream and tried to grab both John and John Jr. in as big a hug as she could manage and hollered, "O, Jesus, save us!" And then promptly vomited all over the two of them.

Well, it was some time before the facts got all sorted out, but I gathered it was merely one of John Jr.'s pranks that backfired: he hadn't counted on his parents being so innocent of what the "transportation of the future" would be like, and *they* could think of nothing else to say but, "O my Lord, it was like the roller coaster at the Fair Grounds in Memphis, only we didn't expect it to go so fast or from so high up. For Heaven's sake, get us back on the ground." And I heard somebody say that Uncle John was heard to murmur, "I'll never get on one of these infernal machines again as long as I live, and you can quote me on that." But Aunt Gladys was already regaining some of her composure, I think: not for nothing had she yearned for this adventure for so many years. But she was determined she would put on the best front possible for the family and all her friends, especially Mary Charlotte McIntosh.

I don't know whether she ever flew again or not; I left home for the navy shortly afterwards. And after the war's end I settled somewhere else and rarely ever went back home. John Jr. later got a Purple Heart because of a wound he received in the South Pacific when one day it suddenly came to him to try flying upside down somewhere over the Great Barrier Reef. And the lurid details of his mother's great adventure above the clouds soon filtered out into the broad landscape back home: she had too big an investment in it to let it die a natural death.

But I was told that, as an "expression" teacher, she had her own dramatic way of presenting the subject to the community, complete with gestures. Her narrative was also inclined to vary from time to time, I heard, apparently according to the mood and temper of her audience. But it always ended the same way: "O, John Jr.'s college graduation was a spectacle to behold, but nothing could ever really compete with his graduation from the air."

The Convertible

Eddie Williams never could decide how he felt about Patricia Carter who lived across the street from him. She was only two months and ten days older than he was, but it was a figure she never forgot and reminded him of it every time she had a chance. He never could figure out what difference it made one way or the other, but she seemed to be very proud of it like it was some achievement for which she and nobody else was responsible and expected to be noticed accordingly every time the clock or the calendar went round. And of course she was a *girl* too, which gave her King's Ex every time she did something she wasn't supposed to or tried to take advantage of Eddie. After all, she said, girls were different from boys: they were *ladies* and deserved to be treated with greater notice than boys and all sorts of privileges granted them that boys didn't have. Unfortunately, most of the other children on Jackson Street, where Eddie and Patricia lived, were also girls, and Eddie had few boys to play with. So he usually felt as though he were some sort of outsider or curiosity with no standing in the community—and of course always having to "give way" to the girls.

Patricia had another advantage too: her mother had died when she was five years old and she didn't even remember her though Eddie did. And she seemed to want to take advantage of this special status also. Eddie always thought that, well, what was it to her? She couldn't very well dwell on it as some sort of perpetual sorrow when she couldn't even remember what her mother looked like. But of course most people naturally felt she was a poor little girl with no mother to guide her along life's weary way and naturally deserved to be taken special notice of and always treated as though she was a "lady," not just another girl who would in due course be a grown woman. And yes, Eddie did think it was unfair: he hadn't had any

particular sorrow—no; but he had tried his best always to behave and
do whatever was his duty, whether in school or elsewhere. And it
looked as if nobody thought the better of him for it either. In some
ways, the whole thing reminded him of the parable of the Prodigal
Son, who had stayed home and behaved himself yet didn't seem to
get any extra credit for it—or Lazarus' sister, Martha, who didn't
seem to get any special attention even from Jesus himself for doing
the dishes after supper, while her sister, Mary, just sat there at His
feet and enjoyed His conversation. To tell the truth, it looked as
though it was usually the sinners that always got the attention—again
like the woman in the Bible who had been forgiven much and was
therefore somehow privileged too.

Later, when he was grown, he felt the same way about what he
thought was the favoritism shown people who didn't pay their bills
or gave trouble in other ways: they got extra credit (certainly, extra
attention) for not doing what they were supposed to do while people
like him were just taken for granted. And, yes, Eddie thought it was
all unfair, even if it did seem authorized by the Lord. And on top of
that he also felt guilty for resenting what he thought was an injustice
even if it did seem to have divine sanction. The world did often seem
to be a very lopsided place which he found difficult to understand:
you sometimes seemed damned if you did and damned if you didn't.
But when one time he asked his mother about it all, she remarked
that it was just one of those things that *had to be*, though nobody
knew exactly why, except it was to show you how the Christian
religion was superior to the others, which were always trying to
balance the books and demanding an eye for an eye and a tooth for
a tooth. *Anybody* could do that, she said, but Christians were
different—and much better—when they returned good for evil. But
all the years when he was growing up it all kept boiling around
inside him; and though he tried to accept the idea and the possibility
that it really might be the order of the day in the hereafter, it just
wouldn't work in the here and now. Really, he thought, it was all
very difficult.

To tell the truth, it always seemed that people like Patricia Carter were pulling rank on whomever they were trying to get ahead of. And this seemed very much the case when Patricia came down with some sort of serious illness when she was in the fifth grade. Naturally, her father, who adored her, took her to the finest set of doctors he could lay his hands on in Memphis, which he was well able to do: he had done very well all these years in the Buick agency. But they just seemed to shake their heads and say it was all beyond them. So Patricia got extra points for that and even more when they took her up to Mayo's Clinic and the folks there said it seemed like some rare blood disease and the prognosis (whatever that was) didn't look too good. But if they could just hold it off for another year or two, they would probably have something that would make it possible to treat it. And meanwhile, Patricia and all her friends and loved ones would just have to pray, which of course Eddie thought would be little satisfaction in the circumstances.

So Patricia came on back home, where she got even more affection and attention than before—really, Eddie thought, like maybe the Catholics treated their saints. And the illness didn't seem to keep her from going on with her life: she could still take tap-dancing lessons and get to be the queen of the Children's Beauty Contest. The main thing was that she just had to take care of herself and not do more than she ought, which again Eddie thought a mighty good excuse for just living to please herself. And of course he felt guilty for that too. In some ways, it always seemed to him that Patricia—and perhaps other girls—always had you in a no-win situation and there was nothing you could do about it.

And this is the way it all went on for some years—Patricia "holding her own," they said, but of course bound to "slip away" one of these days. But naturally she was still getting the thoughts and prayers of everybody in town and even glamorous outsiders too. Like one time when the Life-Saver people brought their circus van through town—all fixed up a la Walt Disney—Mr. Carter persuaded them to drive it down Jackson Street and park it in front of his house so

Patricia could see it without so much commotion and exercise and, O yes, bring little Ethel May Wilkes who had had polio over from across the street so she could have a "private view" also. And Eddie wondered who else they could dig up in the way of the handicapped so as not to leave anybody who was so afflicted out. And of course he knew such thoughts were ugly, but it did seem like the rewards always went to the people who were getting plenty of attention already, with very little left over for just plain down-to-earth folks who were "normal."

And so it went on like that for some years until about the time Patricia and Eddie were in high school. She was still alive, but there was no question that she was getting weaker all the time; apparently Mayo's hadn't yet found any miracle drugs that might help her either. Of course you can't judge the effect illness has on different people, whether in body or in mind; but I had always thought it hadn't sweetened Patricia's spirit any. She was still spoiled, still used to having her own way and still used to being considered "first" in whatever the contest of the moment was. And of course her father would have given her the moon if he could have.

But the way it turned out, he didn't give her the moon; he was about to give her a convertible! This was all back in the forties and fifties, when nothing was considered more fashionable and stylish than a convertible. No matter that they weren't considered the safest things there were: if you turned over in one of them, that was just the end of you, period, and you were just smeared down the highway and that was that. But about the time our crowd was old enough to drive—in the tenth grade or so—the Buick people announced that anybody that wanted a new convertible had better make haste to act because, what with the hardships and scarcities of World War II, they wouldn't be on the market much longer since they were more or less nothing but "luxury" vehicles. And they even sent several samples of the breed to dealers all over the place to let them see what they and their customers might be missing out on if they didn't act now.

So naturally one of them came "on approval" to Mr. Carter—sky-blue and an absolute knockout. And Patricia like to have lost her mind over it. Of course there was no choice for her father: she said he must let her have it right away and no questions asked. According to her, she and the car belonged together—right out of a Hollywood film and glamorous as all get out. And furthermore, she deserved it, after all she had been through these last few years. Of course Eddie heard all about it by remote control, you might say. And he knew Patricia was putting up a strong offense to have her way about it all. But for the first time that Eddie ever knew about, it seemed that Mr. Carter was about to refuse her something she had set her heart on. Why? Eddie didn't really know except what with the drying up of the new automobile market, his sales were not what he was used to. And in fact, he might be on the way to something of a hard time right then. But of course he wasn't the only one: all the merchants around the square were somewhat strapped for cash and everything else that went with it. But Patricia didn't understand it that way: the car just *ought* to have been hers and that was the end of it. Apparently everything else she had ever wanted had been hers for the asking. Why not this one now? And yes, it was a handsome one; Eddie could see Bette Davis, who was always best when she played a bad girl, coming to a cataclysmic, even self-inflicted end in it when the world was, you might say, too much with her—and of course with all possible sound effects to express horror and despair, along with music usually provided for Warner Brothers (her producers) by Max Steiner that Eddie's father always referred to as "killing music," as indicative of what was about to take place. And of course if it wasn't Bette Davis, perhaps Warners' could "borrow" Katharine Hepburn from M-G-M. And yes, Eddie thought, it was as stunning as the moon and all the stars together; and yes, he would have given his eyeteeth for something like it too.

But things in this world don't always work out just as we like: Patricia didn't get the convertible, which finally went to a big cotton planter down in the Mississippi Bottom, and Eddie—and all the others like him—just had to bite their lips too and not shed a tear. Eddie's mother remonstrated with him when he gave signs of such behavior and even told his father he had been taken for a ride in the convertible and it had all gone to his head! And she didn't even seem amused by it as she often did some of his other follies. This was too serious, apparently, and for all she knew, suggested that he didn't have the sense God gave him. And that of course almost brought the tears on for real since it sounded demeaning in every way. Surely, Mr. Carter hadn't talked to Patricia that way: she was *sick* and of course you had to consider her feelings, as usual. They had always come first.

So what happened next? Eddie didn't know what you could call it, but it seemed like some sort of anticlimax. And what was there left for Patricia now? Well, it didn't take so very long to find out because for the next year she showed increasing signs of deterioration—nothing of an appalling nature but just lassitude and decline. And again Mr. Carter took her up to Mayo's to see what they could do for her, but again there was no help. They hadn't even developed the medicine for her ailment they had hoped to, and they still didn't know exactly what she had.

Finally, it became evident that she was dying; it was whispered around town that the Mayo doctors had given her about six months more and that would be it. Whether she knew it herself or not nobody seemed to know; but it was obvious that Mr. Carter knew, he looked so miserable and sad. The end came almost right on the dot Mayo's had predicted too, but Eddie didn't know whether to be heartbroken or mildly amused—it was just almost too coincidental in more ways than one. Things, even death, always seemed to work right on time where Patricia was concerned. And anyway what did it mean? And why had they never found out what her illness was? Furthermore, Eddie had always assumed that somehow God had been on her side all along—because she had always had looks or money or something else to make up for the loss of her mother? Didn't He often provide for people in such contingencies? And did He just make a miscue this time around? Who would ever know?

In any case, Eddie had to go to the funeral: his parents said he had to because good manners required it. So he got all dressed up in his Sunday suit and went over to the funeral home, where the Carter family—what there was left of it—all fell on him like a ton of bricks as someone whom Patricia had always spoken of as her closest friend, maybe even looked forward to him as one day playing a more intimate part in her life. And this of course scared him half to death because he couldn't have imagined such a thing—not only because of Patricia's disposition but also because of his own.

And of course they insisted he come "look" at her, which he was very reluctant to do. But he knew that they were the sort of people who would think they weren't getting their money's worth unless all and sundry came for the exhibition and of course remarked on how "natural" she looked. Anyhow, there she lay, in a delicate blue coffin, wearing an exquisite chiffon dress in much the same shade, a white orchid in one of her hands, and her face now relaxed in something like a sweet, gentle smile. Of course everybody was commenting on how beautiful she looked now. But to Eddie it all looked like nothing so much as a reminiscence of the color and style of the convertible.

The Pickup Truck

This day and time I think all my students—at least the males—want to own and drive a pickup truck. Maybe it's a sign of masculinity or something: I always heard that a sedan was the sign of a tight-welded family, whereas a convertible was a sort of mistress or a kept woman. And I suppose everything has to stand for *something*, but I still wasn't sure about the pickup truck because in the particular case I'm thinking of it wasn't any kind of family car or anything else: it was strictly business and whatever else it was called on to do was just an "extra" or something of the sort. Because the pickup truck I'm thinking of now was as close as we ever came to having a family car, at least until I was almost out of high school.

Because the truck in this case was mostly for use at my father and uncle's hardware store—for deliveries and hauling and fetching and carrying. My uncle and his wife did have a car, mainly I think because she was a schoolteacher and needed one in her job; but my parents—I think now—were saving every penny they could for that far-off time, now drawing ever closer, when I would go off to school. And what they didn't have to spend on the things of this world was to be saved for that. And I realize now it was all admirable and self-less on their part, but as a teenager it was somewhat difficult for me.

And why? Well, nobody can be more vain, self-centered, and downright stupid than an American teenager when he's thinking about the vehicle he wants—indeed, *must* have—when he's old enough to start dating. It's his symbol of position, quality, even, I'm sure, sexual prowess. And though he may have some of the requisites for these things at home or elsewhere, none of them is so visible, so public as what he drives around in. And it goes without saying *he* must do the driving.

Well, what can you do with a pickup truck, in social life or sports or school events or whatever? The answer is not much: it's, for many people, tacky, countrified, all sorts of things that stand on the wrong foot—a symbol of whatever isn't right or elegant or independent and, of course, poverty. And as usual, young people are extremely proud and sensitive to appearances. So what to do? And I should add here that my sensitive situation was compounded further by being the only child of older parents (who were both in their forties when I was born); and they didn't drink or smoke or dance or do any of the fashionable stuff and—I can tell the truth now—I was ashamed of them. Think of having to take a girl out on a date in such a conveyance (this particular one was a Model A Ford, I think, really the pits as some people would now say). Or think of driving to church in it or a traditional school prom—or anywhere else that would speak its own language for itself! It was embarrassment personified.

My parents of course didn't see it that way, and of course that was something I couldn't by any stretch of the imagination understand back then. But of course I do now: it was all a matter of priorities for them. You saved on the things you didn't particularly want or need so you would have the wherewithal for the things that later were to be necessities. But of course young people don't see it that way—not right then. (And of course they never want to *wait*.) I remember one time my mother was laughing because some woman who didn't know her—or the world or anything else—very much had the bad manners to ask her whether she and my father were going to drive up to the Peabody Hotel in Memphis for a meeting (where most of us back then hoped we would go when we died) in the "checkerboard" truck (it was officially painted to suggest Purina feed, for sale of course at the store). And my mother smiled graciously, as only the mannered solvent can do, and said, "Why of course. And the doorman will take my bag up to the front desk, where we'll register, and then on up to our room. That's usually the way, I believe." And no more was said on the subject, I'm sure.

Another time one of the older families in Woodville, who lived in a real *ante bellum* house with columns, were getting ready to marry off one of their daughters, but, at the daughter's request, I think, decreed that there should be no children present for the occasion. (I'm not sure just what lay behind this edict—their fear that children would cause too much commotion or that their mere presence would suggest indelicate matters yet to come—perhaps the "gift and heritage of children," as it said in the *Prayer Book*? Remember, this was a world—back then—which took no notice of children until they were born and ever afterward laid down as revealed gospel that "children should be seen and not heard.") Whatever it was, the wedding was to be held on the great lawn in front of the house, the cedar-lined driveway providing some respite from the fierce August sunshine at that time of day—the late afternoon, with a small chamber orchestra ensconced on the front porch to provide the music and plenty of faithful black retainers in the background to sing a few spirituals to give moral support and then later circulate through the crowd dispensing champagne, beaten biscuits, and country ham. And naturally I had a fit to go and cried real tears when I was told it wouldn't be allowed: even at six years old I had some sense of propriety and resented my apparently not being considered "suitable," or more distressing still, even *left out*. Childhood—as well as adulthood—can have no greater sorrow than that. And children do love any kind of pageantry.

Well, these are but two instances of what I then thought was humiliation, but the worst was yet to come some years later. And that of course was naturally tied in with puberty and the rising sap because it had to do with my first date and the consequences thereof. And it all started when the high school Society of Young Debs announced the plans for their annual Christmas dance. And yes, I got an invitation—have no fear. But of course I was still a chubby teenager and naturally my date had to be the fattest girl in the entire group of freshman pledges.

Of course everybody knew the only way I had to go was in my father's pickup truck (with the checkerboard paint on it), with him at the wheel (because I couldn't drive yet), and me in the middle, and my date, Sara Jane Arnold, tightly wedged against the door. So during the last week of school before Christmas all the Young Debs made a point of sneaking up behind each of us in turn in the cafeteria and measuring our posteriors with a tape measure, then adding up the figures to see whether, along with what they conjectured were my father's generous measurements, we could all fit in that one front seat, then with strident voices proclaiming the latest totals for the benefit of the whole throng.

There may be such things as more embarrassing moments in this our life, but frankly I don't want to know now—or ever—what they are. Even now the memories still burn and roaring rage also, especially against the Young Debs who led the charge. So who could blame me when some years later I, who had by then graduated from college, even taken off a goodly portion of excess weight, and at long last even driven my own car (painted a discreet navy) almost burst into hysterics when I learned that the leader of that pack of Young Debs, usually a girl named Ethel Maud Hendren with freckles and buck teeth and the gall of Lady Macbeth, had married a man that weighed nearly 300 pounds and had a wooden leg? And she said he was one of the best dancers you ever saw; but unfortunately the first time they went to a big dance after they were married his wooden leg—coupled with his 300 pounds—went through the dance floor and at first it looked as though he might be stuck there for the rest of his life. And Ethel Maud herself *did* have hysterics right there at the scene of the crime because, she said, "her sweetie" never would be able to dance again and now her own life was just ruined.

But I bore the whole thing calmly myself and with reason. As it turned out, Sara Jane, my date at that unforgettable Christmas dance, had lost a lot of weight too, but I decided it would take more than that to make me find her at all appetizing. And anyway, my happiest realization now was that whatever else might happen, I wouldn't ever have to go anywhere else in that damned pickup truck.

Stardust

It's strange what people will do when they're trying to be romantic. Of course all the traditional signs and symbols, some of them as tried and true—hackneyed if you like—as all get out. And the rhymes are the same: *June* and *moon* and *croon* and all the rest, and of course, on a lower level, maybe *kiss* and *bliss* thrown in for good measure. There are flowers all over the place too, and of course they have their own harmony. But above all else the beauty of the loved one—and the way it is figured forth are primary. There's Edgar Allan Poe saying the death of a beautiful woman is the most poetical topic there is and then the English, who always seem to find the real beauties blond (because of their Anglo-Saxon heritage?) and the lesser lights (perhaps from southern and eastern Europe) therefore brunette. (In the traditional ballads she's often called "the brown girl.") And these symbols, if that's what you call them, are old hat in that everybody immediately recognizes them for what they are.

Perhaps songs are more difficult to classify, though. And one can spend a lot of time trying to identify their implications, though of course the music itself, to say nothing of the words, can be a very obvious indicator. And of course there are the weather and the landscape too, as in "Deep Purple" and "Stardust"—two of my own favorites. For instance, we (those songs and I) were about the same vintage—born and bred in the thirties, and very much under the influence of romantic movies, where *love* was all. And yes, they all had lovely melodies which you could hum on the way home. (How many such melodies do we have now, and is that a valid criterion any more?) The scenery was standard too: moonlight and roses and nearly everything seen through clouds and mist.

Just how and why all these things became standard I'm not sure: the influence of the impressionists, background music from nineteenth-century composers—all other such things. But the signals were given therewith and, you might say, everybody in the audience more or less got the word, almost like we did from Wagner's and Mendelssohn's wedding music. In short, it may have signified the *customary*, a word which fascinated yet baffled me when I was growing up until my mother finally explained it was something like a symbol, which spared you from having to go into a long song-and-dance en route to get where you were going. And when I asked her whether that was why doctors and nurses usually wore white, she said yes, more or less; and then I understood.

But what about the poetry inherent in the beautiful dead lady? Where and how did that come in? Was there some sort of signal about that too? Perhaps *death* had more to do with enhancing beauty than we might first imagine. Why? Well, because it was fixed and final and there was no going back it somehow gained in worth and value: that's at least part of the surmise—maybe yet another version of the law of supply and demand. And there would be no further changes except inevitable dissolution. No mortal hands could interfere with that process now. And it was frozen forever in eternity. Of course that enhanced its value too. So you had the beauty which was *fixed*, unchanging and unchanged throughout all the ages and never anything else.

But back to my original intent, what was there inherently beautiful or alluring in "Stardust" and all other such essays in the romantic? Would the colors, the shadows, the evening, the stars themselves—all the accompanying machinery—never change but remain fixed always in their significance in that world? Or were they all part of the undying yet somehow ephemeral love that would inevitably delight and yet break the heart—all such things that are both permanent and yet fleeting? Finally, what could be done about the dilemma except dream of the song and the situation it dramatized—all self-contradictory—especially when love and kisses were both new. But that was all long ago now, leaving only the consolation of the stars and the dust they may have left behind, all of them part of the inevitable dream, the inescapable memory. And then we're right back with the standard elements of the drama: a garden wall, the nightingale's fairy tale realized in song, a paradise of roses, and always the memories that preserve the dreams, both words and music.

And that's about it and so far so good. But what are we left with now? As the old question puts it, what can we do for an encore? Is it all just something we can do nothing *with* but fondle over and over in the deep past? Something from eternity we can look back to, as we sit by the fire, something we can hold on to down the ages? But again, what will be our reward—something we can possess forever and never lose, and the melody, with its refrain, the stardust itself remain with us always? And will that be enough to keep our hearts intact?

Well, it all sounds pretty sentimental, and perhaps we must ask ourselves whether we can stomach it all now and from this on out? And if so how and why? Well, perhaps we can because it celebrates the beauty, the love, intangible of course, which always lasts because it depends on nothing external, nothing of this world to keep it going. Perhaps it's like Keats's odes—the nightingale's song, the beauty in all the arts, like the Grecian urn, and the everlasting autumnal scene which finally brings us quiet joy and peace and needs no explanation. Finally there are the lovers in *The Eve of St. Agnes* who ride away into the night, ultimately into death but somehow last forever too: what have they gained, what have they lost? Can anyone really say? Perhaps not, only that they were given it once before and now yet again—but this time for always.

I've Got a Sneaking Idea That . . .
or
I'd Just Get Me a Lawyer

I don't suppose there's ever been a woman more plainspoken and down to earth than my mother. Not that she used rude or even rough language; indeed she was one of the most tactful people I ever knew. (She always prefaced *suspicions* but not *facts* with "I've got a sneaking idea that. . . . ") But when it was called for, she just told it like it was and you could take it or leave it. Furthermore, she made no bones—in suitable company—about her likes and dislikes.

Yes, she thought women were smarter than men—at any rate, smarter about *folks*. (It was men that were more likely to make fools of themselves, with their big ideas and ambitious schemes.) But at the same time men had no monopoly on foolishness. And I guess it's all summed up in her comment on women who were always running off to consult their preachers or a counselor or an analyst or whatever about what to do if they were in any kind of trouble or needed advice of any kind, whether worldly or spiritual. Once, I know, I called her hand on the subject and asked her what she would do if *she* felt the need of advice or spiritual guidance. But that didn't faze her a bit: she just snorted and in a very peremptory manner replied, "Humph! I'd just get me a lawyer!" And that was that.

And I knew she meant every word of it too—just like she did when one of the local beauty "operators" had an unexpected turn of good luck. (Her name was Violet Savage, which sounds like a name concocted by Evelyn Waugh, and she worked at the Elite Beauty Parlor down on the square right next to the picture show, and her specialty was "machineless" permanent waves that used clamps on the rolls of curls instead of electricity, which made all the about-to-be curls emit steam and frying noises to boot—and somehow always made me think of the Spanish Inquisition. But this was all before there was anything like the do-it-yourself-at-home kind of "cold wave" that appeared on the scene toward the end of World War II.) Well, anyway, Violet's good luck happened to her when the married man she had been going with on the side for years and years suddenly lost his wife and everybody around town felt that paved the way for them to get married after a "decent interval." Not that they thought this would "make an honest woman" of her overnight, but at least it would terminate her living in sin for the rest of her life.

I remember the night after her predecessor's death—whose body was now on display for the "visitation" up at the funeral home, with a big marquee out front to tell you exactly who was dead and when the funeral would be—my father saw skyrockets being set off down on the square but forgot that it was the Fourth of July, so he came home and told my mother, with something of a diabolical grin, it was obviously Violet's boy friend celebrating.

Well, that kind of humor ran in the family, but I just contented myself with remarking loftily that you just never knew *what* each day might bring (like a member of my mother's bridge club that just keeled over dead on the kitchen floor one afternoon while she was making watermelon rind pickles). And with some dramatic flair I remarked that Violet must have been absolutely flabbergasted to think her difficult situation had now been set right so unexpectedly, in the twinkling of a eye or a thief in the night, you might say, and *who* would ever know just how she felt *now*? Well, my mother was sitting there in the living room reading a continued story entitled "Look Eastward to the Morning"—which she freely admitted was a lot of junk but at least harmless—in the current *Ladies' Home Journal*; and she didn't even bother to look up from the page but merely observed, "Better," and went right on with her reading.

Because she was the last person on earth to cry over spilt milk. If you could mend it, then do it; but if that was impossible, you just had to go on with your rat killing and that was that. And stouthearted

Christian woman that she was, she was still thoroughly at home in the world, like she was about getting a lawyer if you needed advice. On the whole, she didn't seem to put much faith in preachers and such like. Whether she thought them too unworldly I don't know; but I know she didn't have any illusions about *them*. Because really, she didn't have a lot of confidence in men; and she often quoted her Great-aunt Ida Mae to the effect that there wasn't a man in captivity that you could really trust below the belt.

I suppose she figured that well, if you really needed or wanted advice, a lawyer would be your best bet because at least you went to see him with your eyes open and knew what you were getting into: it was *business* and the last thing any sensible person would want at such a time was *sympathy*. (My father had always said that when anybody died and somebody asked how much money had left, well, it really didn't make much difference because the lawyers and other thieves would get most of it.)

In any case, neither of them believed in Santa Claus, not even the one who wrote "Yes, Virginia." And I remember my mother saying she would be ashamed to tell it that she had had to take her oldest child out behind the house and whisper in his ear who and what the jolly old elf was really all about. Because the family had had to do something like that for my father's oldest brother—Uncle John, the preacher—when he was already in his teens and no wonder then that you couldn't expect anybody like that to be very much at home in the world. In fact, most of the preachers she had ever known, she said, just seemed to think all you had to do was calmly sit in the swing on the front porch with your hands folded and God would provide. (They didn't seem to believe that God had given you sense and He expected you to *use* it.) And as for herself, she had always had a dubious opinion about the Sermon on the Mount: she hated to think what would have happened to *her* if she had tried to behave like a lily of the field. And if she hadn't toiled and spun most of her life, she didn't think she would have ever made anybody think of Solomon in all his glory, much less the Queen of Sheba. As for fowls of the air and so on, she was inclined to think the Lord expected you to have gumption enough to fend for yourself—or else you'd starve to death.

It was all part of what you had to do, she thought, not only to stay alive but also to keep the world in motion. Like Jesus rebuking Martha for being put out with Mary for not helping her was the dishes: she always said she was disappointed in Him for saying that. Of course *somebody* had to do it. And you couldn't expect people to just sit around the house entertaining company all the time. And then what in the world were you to think of the prodigal son, who fared just as well as the older brother? I'm pretty sure she thought that whole business was unfair.

I imagine my mother also had her doubts about the concept of "holy waste" too, when you poured oil over Him whom you honored and revered—not because she was tightfisted or selfish but, she might have asked, what good would it do? Maybe she was even somewhat like the old miser in one of Scott's novels who, on his deathbed, forbade his survivors to put more than one candle beside his bed because, he said, one candle was enough to die by. She was nothing if not practical though thoroughly at home with God, only sometimes not altogether in perfect agreement with Him.

But yes, you had to render unto Caesar that which was his and also make to yourself friends of the mammon of unrighteousness, maybe even the unjust steward too. You might find it somewhat uncomfortable at times; perhaps thee would even be times when you just didn't like it. But were there not also times which made provision for both the children of this world and the children of light too?

The Little Girl with the Blue Eyes

In the photograph she stands, a little girl about five years old, clutching her doll in one hand and her cat in the other. Her blond hair explodes into ringlets—naturally curly; and she is dressed in what looks like her Sunday best: a long dress—full-skirted and almost touching the ground, with puffed sleeves and lots of rick-rack for trimming. It's hard to know precisely of course since the original picture was old and faded, but many years ago I took it to a photographic studio to be "restored" and that is what emerged from the old print. I told the young woman who waited on me at the studio that I didn't want them to dress up the photograph, just restore it, in color, so that it would be clear and fresh. And this was the result. Her dress is red, her cat is gray, and her eyes are blue: the latter was the only thing I could be sure of—always the blue eyes. The other colors were just a guess. But the eyes were blue: I was firm about that. Because she was my mother, and always people—both within and outside the family—remembered her eyes—the brightest blue you can imagine, almost like cornflowers. And in the photograph they dazzle you, as winning and loving as ever. One of the cousins even used to call her "Miss Blue Eyes," but of course her name was Lillian.

I never could make up my mind about that: Lillian wasn't what I would have called a tacky name like Viola or a comfortable name like Bessie, and it wasn't elegant like Elizabeth. It had probably been fashionable—back when people were reading Tennyson all over the place—sounding perhaps far-off and romantic. But at least it wasn't Vivien or Elaine. And it had dated, by the time I came along.

But the photograph was something I always cherished. For one thing, it had been taken by my father's oldest brother, Uncle John. And he said he had always considered that photograph of my mother one of his masterpieces. I never knew why exactly. It was of course taken years before anybody ever thought of marrying into the Drake family; but of course her family—the Woods—and the Drakes had known each other always—out at Maple Grove, the community three miles southeast from Woodville where they all grew up. And my mother and father had many relatives in common but weren't actually kin themselves, which fact used always to fascinate me for some reason. *Kinfolks* were almost a mystique in that world, where I grew up, some forty years ago in the rural South; and I know the word always had some special distinction for me—describing a strange and baffling mystery which was all a part of your own self, your background, your past. And like it or not, there wasn't anything you could do about it: one old soul of our acquaintance even observed that God gave you kinfolks but, thank the Lord, you could choose your friends.

But the idea that my mother had once been a little girl—four or five years old—and standing there with her dolly and her kitty, to have her picture taken, was fascinating, if somewhat incomprehensible, to me when I first saw the photograph as a child. I was a child, and she was my mother. Between us there yawned a vast and unbridgeable tract of years. It was hard to think of her as ever being a child, loving, needing to be loved, her blue eyes, which were still so distinctive, looking toward the outside world with something like both delight and fear. But she had been a little girl; and my father, when he was especially pleased or amused with something she had said or done, would always shake his head in delight and say, "Mama's just like a little girl, so full of laughter and mischief."

And that was something else: to him, she was both "Mama" and a little girl. How could that be? I knew my parents never called each other by their Christian names: she was always "Mama" at home or, to outsiders, "Miss Lillian," and he was always "Daddy" or else "Jucks," which was his nickname. I think she had, when they first married, tried calling him by his Christian name, which was the same as my own. But hardly anyone else in the world did that, and she finally gave up. Could they not bear to see themselves, just as they were, in their grown-up bodies and natures" Did they have to have the protective covering of other names, names which suggested that somehow they were playing at adulthood and family life? I'll never know, I suppose. Certainly, in that time and place, there were many couples who shrank from the open intimacy of first names: my Aunt Estelle bore Uncle John three children and still, after fifty years of marriage, called him "Mr. Drake."

But I think always that Dad preferred to think of Mama as the little girl—maybe even the little girl with the kitty and the dolly—that he could both pet and spoil. Because that's of course what he did. She never learned to drive: he was always there to drive her. He and my Uncle Buford, his youngest brother, owned their own store and were their own masters, so she would call him to come home at any time of the day if she were feeling lonesome or blue. And of course he was always there, to run errands for her, to do whatever she asked.

Because that was the other side of the coin from the little girl in the photograph: she was still a little girl and needed very much to be loved and cherished. But, in her dealings with me, my mother was anything but the little girl: she was firm and authoritative in all her opinions and judgments, and from them there was no appeal. I knew I could nearly always get round my father, but not her. And it was hard to think of my mother as ever being as defenseless in her love, clutching the dolly and the kitty close as if for aid and comfort, as she seemed in that photograph.

I knew that, after her parents died—so close together, she had gone to live with an aunt and had taken a job in a dentist's office downtown and more or less been an independent person. And I've often thought what a really terrible crisis she had to go through at that time—her home broken up, being turned out into the world, more or less on her own, so suddenly, though of course she was grown. And I wondered, as I was growing up and came to know more about her, what such an experience had done to her. Something, I felt sure. The little girl in the photograph had had her playhouse destroyed: no mother or father, no home, her kitty and dolly so use-less now. And yet something remained. There were still the blue eyes, and they were as winning—and loving or needing love—as ever. Or that's what I thought must have been the case.

Because that was one of the reasons, I thought, why my father married her. The blue eyes, so full of love and care, but no dolly, no kitty now; and she needed somebody to look after her. And he delighted in doing it. He had recently lost his own mother, whom he had adored; and thus I think my mother became at once wife and lover and mother to him. I'm sure they neither of them would ever have thought of it in those terms: probably they would have been scandalized at the very idea. But something like this, I think, always lay at the heart of their relationship. And, remember, she called him "Daddy" too; and I don't think that was just for my benefit either. He did become a kind of surrogate father for the real one she had loved and lost. His father, her mother ran poor seconds in such matters, though they both seemed to cherish the greatest affection in them.

They had been married eight years when I was born, and I gather they had wanted a child badly. They were both middle-aged by then: she was forty and he was forty-five. And when I was growing up, that was a source of discomfort, even shame to me: all my friends had young parents that smoked and drank and danced and did God knows what else, and there I was saddled with what I thought were a couple of old fogies. And I suppose I was ashamed at the thought that I was the product of old people's passion, of middle-aged lusts. It all somehow seemed unsuitable, even indelicate. And I had no grandparents, except for an ancient paternal grandfather who was a Confederate veteran: that's how old *he* was. My parents could have been my grandparents: they were old enough. And sometimes I thought they were trying to raise me that way—out-of-date, out-of-step with the times, as I thought they were. No first names with them: I had to say always "sir" and "ma'am" and of course never any bald, naked Christian names used to or about other adults. It always had to be "Mr." and "Miss," which in turn might, if I knew them well enough, be followed by a Christian name rather than a surname. But always the ceremonial forms had to be observed.

And I suppose it was natural that I should grow up with the past ever present in my world. It swirled around me continually in the talk of my parents and their families—particularly my father's—and their friends; and it was always treated as something still very much alive and highly influential. It never occurred to me then that the past was over and done with or dead—or that anyone might think it was. The past—and the characters and their actions which made it up—were realities to my parents and forever present all about them, as was the tradition of talk. And I learned early to keep my mouth shut and my ears open. How many times I was told "Children should be seen and not heard" or, as they looked at each other over my head. Both literally and figuratively, "Little pitchers have big ears!" and I hated them for it, while at the same time I longed for the day when I could enter into their world of adulthood, their world of talk, even their world of the past. After all, I hardly had any past of my own—and wouldn't until I was grown. Perhaps that would be the common denominator between me and them. So I both though and acted older than I was, to the chagrin of my contemporaries and, I now suspect, the dismay of my parents.

Well, I did grow older in time; and, to some extent, I was able to come to terms with my parents, if not on a basis of equality, then at least with some concession, on their part, that I had reached years of discretion and was of age, as they say. But things didn't altogether turn out as I had planned. My mother fell ill, some years before my father's death, with what then was termed a nervous breakdown and had to be hospitalized because of her extreme depression. (I learned later that it was more or less precipitated by menopause.) And during this time she grew increasingly more dependent on my father and more and more possessive toward me, as she wailed that she would be better off dead but had no idea of what would happen to us if she were. It was all a painful ordeal not only for her but for us—and especially me, who was a teenager.

I think I realized then, for the first time, how perilous love could be and how tyrannical and destructive. For my mother became more and more the little girl with the blue eyes, clutching at both my father and me—no dolly or kitty to cling to now. And her eyes were as blue as ever but had somehow lost their luster. I know it almost broke my father's heart, to see her so miserable; but he stayed behind her through it all and pushed and pulled her back into some degree of health within a year. I didn't realize it then—luckily—but this was the first of a series of such illnesses for her. And after my father died, very suddenly, when I was off at college, she grew worse. She would cry and wring her hands and say, again and again, "There's no one to scotch for me any more, now that Daddy's gone." And I both pitied and despised her for her weakness: it was hard for me to think of it as just another illness. Was she still the little girl with the blue eyes in the photograph? Looking tentatively about her, fearful that her love would not be returned by someone, anyone who might be near? Did she miss the dolly and the kitty even more than ever?

I know that, in her last illness, after years of both mental and physical debilitation, she would cling, with a surprisingly strong grip, to my hand when I would go to sit with her in the hospital and ask me again and again whether I still loved her. I supposed that was better—but not much—than her tears and pleas to be allowed to go home during the previous years when she had been a patient in a state hospital. But all the nurses loved her and said how pretty she still was—her hair snow-white now but still curly, her eyes as blue as ever if somewhat bleared. And I suppose they wondered why I wasn't more demonstrative and outwardly affectionate. Perhaps I was still afraid of the blue eyes, the little girl in the photograph—their terrible defenseless need for love and yet their terrible strength in such weakness. I worried about it considerably but had to play the game all the way out by the rules I had laid down years before. I would do everything for her I could, but she would not possess me, even destroy me as I suspected she had my father. Not that he was unwilling, for which I perhaps unconsciously despised him. It had been his choice, but I accused him in my heart of weakness, I suppose. But no, she was not going to take me with her, to the grave or into the past, or anywhere else. I had my own life to lead and must lead it on my own terms.

A day or two before she died, I arrived at the hospital just as the nurses were changing shifts, as I usually managed to do, so I could talk to both of them about my mother's condition. And I know, as we stood there in the sterile gray corridor, I kept asking them how much longer did they think she would linger—to suffer what I thought had already been indecently too much; and also I know I wanted it all over and done with—to end her suffering and (I might as well face facts) also my own. I wasn't too proud of my seeming coldness towards her now. At one time, it might have been necessary for self-protection but surely not any more. Still, the defenseless little girl with the blue eyes and the curly hair preyed on my thoughts: had she never been loved enough, protected enough, sheltered enough? But was I the one to do it? Had my father been right to try? It was one of those enigmatic puzzles that you could never solve. At any rate, in the midst of my thoughts while talking to the nurse, one of them— the day nurse, I think—said, "You know, a lot of old people, when they come to die, are ready to go. But your mother wants to live. And she grips my hand and asks me whether I love her, and of course I say I do. But it's really only you that she loves. God only knows how much she loves you." To which I replied, yes, I knew that. And I turned away so they wouldn't see the tears in my eyes at my thoughts, the judgment I was passing on myself.

With all its perils, had I risked enough to love her properly? Had I been always too afraid of the charm of the blue eyes and the curly hair, the little girl with the dolly and the kitty? Destructive or not, she had loved, she had risked, and she had paid a terrible price for what she had ventured. Had I been rendered incapable of love by such power as was manifested in hers, and whose fault was it anyway? Not altogether hers, I was sure. Had I fought back enough or too much? Had I even tried to love her in return, or had I merely withdrawn into my shell and refused the danger, the opportunity? I was a loser, whichever way in turned, it seemed. It was all a muddle—and a sad one.

I stood there in the hallway pondering it all until the day nurse had collected her things and left; then I joined the other nurse in my mother's room. My mother seemed to be resting comfortably; perhaps she was asleep. But it made no difference. I went over to her bed, took her hand in mine and bent down and whispered, "It's me, Mamma. I'm here."

Robert Drake

Traveling Companions

One of the delights for me when I visited London in the old days was reading *The Times* every morning, especially the personals columns, which then occupied the front page, quite properly relegating the news of the day, the fashions of the hour, or the modes of the moment to the deep interior within, not far from the "leading articles," as they called the editorials, where such things belong. After all, what could the latest atrocities from some supposedly civilized nation—bombings, rapes, riots, the death rattle of Western civilization itself, or even the birth pangs of a so-called emerging nation—what could any of them offer to compare with the human interest (what is *inhuman* interest unless it's such horrors?), the implied dramas, the fanciful speculations conjured up by such items as "Sister" Allan's offering to give enemas ("colonic irrigations," they were called) to any and all throughout greater London (nights included) or Miss Gem Moufflet's announcing her availability for tuition in ballroom dancing, either in class or in private?

And these examples were only the most engaging in a long series of items such as "Darling Ruth, I still love you even on our Silver Anniversary, Ted" or "John, I didn't really mean it. Please come back. Love, Mary," and other communications public and private— my all-time favorite, however, remaining "For sale: wedding dress and veil, greatly reduced. Never worn." Of course these supposedly private communications, the personals, became as public as *The Times* itself; and yet there was something engaging, almost touching in the intimacies so publicly revealed and yet still protected and inviolate. (No names were given, just telephone numbers and maybe on occasion a *Times* "post box" address.) Did their perpetrators and their audiences all turn a blind eye to such delicate subjects, with the left hand trying not to know what the right hand was doing, in some sort of unstated agreement to respect the most-private revelations, the most-personal offers to buy and sell? Whatever the case, I loved it all—very human and of course very English.

It's all different now, though. The personals are found on the back pages of *The Times*, with the news occupying the front, like any other journal; and they're not so numerous—or so "personal"—as in the old days. And Sister Allan and Miss Gem Moufflet have departed this venue if not this life. (I had thought, with their particular talents, they might be immortal.) The court circular still appears just after the editorial page, along with "Today's Arrangements," which makes public that day's royal engagements; and I'm sure that, if our civilization were coming to an end tomorrow, whether with a bang or a whimper, it would be announced therein that the queen, accompanied by the duke of Edinburgh, would be present for this literally ultimate event, with the Lord X and the Lady Y in attendance, and nobody would turn a hair. (Yes, there'll always be an England. And yes, I've often thought this kind of discipline, this respect for form is what civilization means, and yes, punctuality *is* the politeness of kings.)

But anyhow the personals just aren't what they used to be—now mostly offers to rent villas on the Mediterranean, sell "previously owned," even—shudder—"secondhand" cars (But rarely Rolls-Royces or Bentleys these days—who can afford them now, new or old?). And of course there are trumpetings of packaged "holidays," never "vacations." (Villa parties? singles cruises?—you name it—on the Costa del Sol or the isles of Greece?) All rather humdrum now, and one wonders whether the erstwhile reading public gets its *frissons* these days from some other source. Perhaps so much of what was formerly considered indelicate or even scandalous has become so "public," indeed so common, in every sense of the word, it's lost even the power to titillate. In any case, all those with what I believe the French call "special tastes" (but not necessarily with salacious overtones) must mourn its passing.

The English of course, with their climate, are often obsessed with the idea of keeping warm and dry; so at the first signs of the sun's reappearance after an absence of some length they will immediately make for the outdoors, as I remember very well when I was once a guest at a full-dress dinner party as part of a real-live English country-house weekend. And yes, I had even had my suitcase unpacked on arrival by one of the servants; and the men did linger at the dinner table, after the ladies had "withdrawn," to smoke cigars, drink their brandy, and of course engage in "low" conversation until the host gave the customary signal: "Shall we join the ladies?"

But of course our meal itself had actually taken place in the exquisite walled garden, complete with roses and other *flora* (I can't remember any herbaceous borders, though) burgeoning riotously in the romantic June twilight, the grass still sopping wet after a fierce late afternoon shower, with a stiff gale making the lighted candles on the table struggle to survive, and a temperature which must have been hovering not many degrees above freezing because, according to our hostess, she *always* had to take advantage of the good weather *whenever* it came. So she had thoughtfully provided the ladies with scarves and shawls to wear over their summer-weight dinner dresses but, unfortunately, had nothing for the relief of the dinner-jacketed men, who had to show their spunk by keeping stiff upper lips and freezing quietly in the dusk. But there were some saving graces: the food was very good; and the wine, chosen with impeccable discrimination, helped to keep us warm. And breakfast in bed the next morning helped to cover a multitude of whatever other sins were left over.

✳ ✳ ✳

But I digress. No, the personals in *The Times* are not what they used to be. And I long for the old days of "Titled lady requires . . . " or even—a step down of course—"Titled lady offers. . . . " And gone with the wind indeed are what I always considered the most delightfully brazen of all: items beginning with "Public school man available. . . . " *The Times* itself doesn't seem quite the same, and to risk a tasteless pun, perhaps the times themselves are out of joint.

But I'm not altogether despairing, in fact, somewhat heartened, because of an advertisement I saw in the personals columns during my most recent visit to London just a few weeks ago. And it read:

Traveling Companion

Well presented businessman in early 30's on holiday in England seeks equally well presented and attractive lady to tour England by car for approximately 5 to 7 days. Will pay part or all expenses. This offer attaches no undisclosed obligations.

Then a telephone number and the hours during which calls would be accepted during the following days were given. And the item ended with the stern admonition to call at "NO OTHER TIMES."

This offer, this personal, can certainly hold its own with either Sister Allan or Miss Gem Moufflet; but in these latter days such manifestations of the old spirit are rare. I need hardly say how much my attention was arrested by the announcement, what flights of fancy it gave rise to. Indeed, so bizarre did it seem—especially the injunction against calling at any but the specific times—that one of my American friends to whom I showed it was convinced it was a message in code relating to the international white slave traffic. But aside from the "well presented" requisite vaunted and then in turn demanded (what *did* it mean—that you dressed in good taste, didn't dye your hair, or still had the teeth God gave you?), what fascinated me most was the phrase "TRAVELING COMPANION."

And I was reminded at once of a song I had heard Beatrice Lillie sing years ago, when she was performing in a program of skits for two actors, along with Reginald Gardiner, who, among other things, was doing imitations of wallpaper—the kind with large red roses climbing on a trellis in precise geometrical patterns, just the kind some people who suffer from obsessive-compulsive disorders feel often compelled to count. Anyhow, if my memory doesn't fail me, one of Miss Lillie's triumphs was a rather plaintive ditty entitled

"Not Wanted on the Voyage." And some of the verses went something like this: "Everyone's got traveling companions, / And they're sticking to them like glue [pronounced of course 'glew'] / But *I'm* not wanted on the voyage." Then later on, summing it all up: "Nobody wants this old bag." And more in that inimitable vein.

Alas for the days of the great grand ocean liners and their elegant passengers (at least in first class) with mounds of luggage, some to be taken with them in the cabin, the rest stowed in the hold because, as the label read, they were "NOT WANTED ON THE VOYAGE." Alas for those golden times, alas for our unglamorous present (our airline luggage originally limited to a mere 44 pounds—66 in first class, I believe). And alas for all of us, with so little space, so little time for quality, even life itself under such dreary conditions. Not even the Concorde, with all its speed faster than sound, can compete with that: its affluent passengers are all cramped together in that thin, elongated cabin that looks like some sort of test tube and when the sound does catch up with the speed, I'm inclined to think it affects even us far, far below almost literally like the crack of doom.

I'm not sure that speed in and of itself can ever masquerade as *style*, which depends more on a sort of deliberate and carefully orchestrated languor. And anything that betokens *haste* is unseemly, to say the least: style belongs, almost by definition, to those who don't have to hurry. And if we really want to play the game all the way out, we can ask ourselves what it is that flying itself can offer us except speed? There can be few amenities in such cramped quarters, little quietude and relaxation in the midst of such noise, few "sights" beneath the clouds, and finally no real pleasure, as a friend of mine once remarked, in travel that is only *transit*.

Well, I don't want to wallow in gloom here; but traveling companions are a serious matter, and the subject should not be lightly treated. (I've even suspected that they may, along with money, be the ultimate test—of friendship, of affection, really of almost any human value: whom would you want to travel with, for short trips or long, even through life itself, and how much would it be worth, however measured?) The *Times'* well-presented businessman, Miss Lillie's comic song, both really concern the same thing: everybody needs a traveling companion, no matter who he is or where he's headed, whether lost in the mazes of sorrow and suffering or marching gaily down the broad highway of life. We can't do without one really, whether we demand one on terms of our own choosing—like the *Times* advertiser, but remember, he was willing to pay too—or indeed feel, like Beatrice herself, that we've been relegated to the hold because nobody wants us. But a traveling companion we must have.

And this is what, I suppose, leads to some of the peculiar arrangements one sees these days. I wasn't born yesterday, but I hope I don't sound antediluvian when I say that the people some folks pick out to get attached to often seem very strange choices to me. And I'm not necessarily talking about marrying a spouse with a harelip or a wooden leg or anything like that. As a matter of fact, I knew of an old lady over in Arkansas who had been married twice, each time to a man with a wooden leg, the first of whom she said was one of the best dancers you ever saw in your life. (Unfortunately, I never found out what charms the second one had.) And the mother of the two girls, my contemporaries, from Kentucky who used to visit their grandmother next door to us every summer was an undertaker who played the violin. But the grandmother took it all in her stride. It was merely one of those things—burying people—that just *had to be done*, with or without a violin, she said; and that's all there was to it.

Perhaps all such personals, then, are cries of distress, signals that a traveling companion is needed somewhere by somebody. perhaps the companion desired is not even human: it may well be the glamorous automobile or the villa on the Mediterranean, whatever gives us the feeling that we are worth something, whether in affection or hard cash. But we matter. And usually, we want to matter to someone else. Even today, with the explicit, even lurid "want ads" (not in the *Times* of course) asking for thinly veiled forms of sexual gratification—even stating exactly what it is the vendors have that will prove desirable to the prospective "buyer," it's the same thing—a plea for attention, a kind of SOS that says: "I have something you want, something you need, even though you may not know it, and we can make each other happy if we want to." Sometimes it's sad, sometimes it's funny, the length—or the depths—human beings will go to in their need, their loneliness. But I think, somehow, we must take them seriously, if only to see, which is to say listen, to what it is they're asking for. Who knows what widened horizons, what opportunities for self-fulfillment such a response will finally create for us all?

The Cotton Mill

The first time I ever went to England was in the late 1950s—when the great ocean liners still plied the waters of the Atlantic and Cunard (the line of the Queens and the *Mauretania*, which I was traveling on) proudly carried as one of its watchwords "Getting There Is Half the Fun." And it was too—just like being in a great resort hotel out in some vast tract of land, with all the horizon around you and nothing to do but what was pleasing: eat, drink, read, play any number of games, and of course make new friends anywhere they surfaced. Indeed, you might have said it was not unlike transcontinental rail travel back in the golden age several decades ago; but now of course hardly any of the young people I teach have ever been on a train, much less an ocean liner.

I found, incidentally, to my surprise, that ocean travel usually brought out the best in people: you were all out there in the middle of the ocean and you really could hardly afford not to be civil. It was like a desert island in some respects: you couldn't just get up and run off if you didn't like it. And also it put you on your good behavior in your own surroundings, your own demeanor. Where you were from, how you would act were matters of great importance; and much depended on whether you kept your manners gracious and all went smoothly. Out there, in the middle of the sea, you were only what you made out of yourself; and other people, you might say, were playing solitaire too, responsible to nobody but themselves for their own appearance and conduct. And there was no coaching from the sidelines, whether from relatives or friends either. You were on your own now.

Well, as I said, this was my first such trip, and I was determined to mind my Ps and Qs, and if not actually being cited at the end of the voyage as "Mr. Congeniality at Sea", at least not cause any commotion. And I suppose I hadn't thought anyone else would think of doing otherwise. But unfortunately, I was still young and inexperienced; and I really didn't know what snares and delusions might be open to the first-time voyager.

So I was taken a good deal by surprise when I encountered a couple from a large town only twenty miles or so from my own home in Woodville, Tennessee—them and their two adolescent children, boy and girl. But they, who gave me to understand right off that they were—and always had been—great and big-time travelers, made haste to identify themselves in more ways than one. Of course they knew West Tennessee, though they had not grown up there but rather in the Midwest, where everybody was sentenced to roll his Rs and harden his vowels for life, which of course was obvious the first time they opened their mouths. And they had to drive through Woodville every time they went south to Memphis—that wonderful metropolis fifty miles away where most of us from that part of the country thought we would go when we died and maybe even get to stay at the Peabody Hotel—that is, if we had behaved ourselves.

So of course we went through the usual formula of "do you know so-and-so" up and down the highway all the way to the big city, naturally climaxing in Memphis itself, where there were people who had traveled too and knew where they were and of course might have the last word on you too. And not for the first time was I made aware that it really was a small world.

Well, that didn't particularly disturb me: I had always been taught to behave myself and not to forget where and how I had been brought up—not that others didn't also have "backgrounds" too. After all, you weren't traveling just to show off and alert the general public to your origins then and your whereabouts now. But I found out soon enough that such things did matter a great deal to these, my neighbors north of Woodville. It was quite obvious that they were well-to-do, not that they proclaimed it to all and sundry but mainly in the allusions they made and references they dropped—where they bought their clothes, where they vacationed (naturally Florida, but up in what people called the "Redneck Riviera" around Pensacola, which signaled to me the possibility that they might not be so high on the hog after all).

Of course they assumed that all of us aboard would want to know where they were planning to send their children when they went off to school, but they just hadn't decided yet and anyway they still had two or three high-school years ahead of them. And of course you couldn't be too careful about making choices about such things. Finally, they were familiar with all the signs and signals which Americans knew how to display—very casually of course—when they traveled: unlike some Europeans, they never felt the need to rely on a class system.

I wasn't altogether a babe in the woods about such matters either; I had had some foretaste of such paraphernalia in my limited travel around the United States, but had never thought it made a whole world of difference. People could use the eyes and ears God had given them and would find out most of what there was to know about you soon enough without your proclaiming it. But that didn't seem enough for the Goodsons, as I soon found out my new acquaintances were called. Yes, and their pedigrees too: DAR, UDC, Country Clubs, and the usual. But how were they to make public their finances without being really vulgar? Well, it didn't take long to find out when some mention was made at our dinner table of how and where we lived. Cunard had put several of us Southerners at the same table in the dining room, I thought perhaps to cement our relationship as compatriots and cut down on any sectional friction which might still be lingering on, lo these many years after "the War."

But perhaps they got more than they bargained for because some of those same fellow travelers seemed to take a lot of pleasure in discussing the food we were having: yes, they had had some of the same "foreign" dishes we were eating now before—but much better prepared, they said—and anyway, they had no particular interest in anything that came out of the sea or was fried and *never* touched gravies, sauces, or anything else which suggested overseas provenience. And

I thought immediately of my father's comments about those who always advertised their likes and dislikes about such matters in public: he said you could tell right away they had all been raised on branch water.

I learned very quickly too that the Goodsons at least were big cotton farmers, maybe even what, in the old days, would have been called *planters*. Well, I thought I could survive that piece of information because as things were going these days, raising cotton was getting more and more expensive—because of the necessary machinery involved and of course because there was no cheap labor available, white or black (what used to be called sharecroppers). And my father, who years before couldn't have imagined anybody farming who didn't raise cotton, said he was glad to turn over a new leaf and take up soybeans; and *that* had been some time ago and, for that matter, hadn't caused any particular kind of hullabaloo. (The son of a Confederate veteran, a Virginian who had been at Appomattox, he was something of a conservative in his politics. But I knew him well enough by then to remember that he always said you couldn't be an ostrich: you had to move with the times.)

But in my ignorance I hadn't really thought much about such matters; for one thing, I was still too young—just graduated from college and planning to enter graduate school in the fall. And the main thing I knew about cotton and its logistics was that it wasn't for the fainthearted. The crop inevitably entailed the ownership of—or heavy investment in—expensive equipment, even a gin if it was done on a big enough scale. And of course there were the numerous pitfalls of dealing with cotton buyers and stewing about the vagaries of the market and all sorts of hazards where you could "lose everything you had" and then some—especially if you got involved with those unmentionable—and probably unscrupulous—operators who "dealt in cotton futures," which always sounded extremely sinister but I didn't know much more than that.

So as soon as the dinner table conversation came around to the ways and means of cotton farming and how it could be turned into a fortune if you knew your business and how it was still, after all these years, the way for "quality" to live, I felt very much over my head and thought how good it would be if we could just somehow, without causing too much disturbance, change the topic of conversation. So I just spoke up and said, in all my ignorance, "Well, my father says he's worn out with raising cotton: it's all too uncertain and costs too much to raise anyhow. So now he just has soybeans." Which then was followed by a silence you could have cut with a knife before the Goodsons vouchsafed, almost in unison, "Well, *we* are the cotton mill in our town. And everywhere we go people seem to know right off who we are just because of that. It wasn't called 'King Cotton' back in the old days for nothing, you know." And of course I didn't know any better than to try pulling my foot out of my mouth all by myself. So I up and replied that well, my father preferred soybeans as his main crop, if for no other reason than cotton's forcing you to deal with so much manual labor in the fields. Everybody knew, he had said, that it wouldn't be too long now before machines would be taking over most of the work, and cotton would be no exception. Therefore he thought he would get ahead of the changes that were coming right now before it went any further. But, alas, that led to further silence.

It was obvious that I had made some awful kind of *gaffe* or, as my mother would have put it, a real *let* and, as a result, might be transported to a penal colony or handed over to Scotland Yard as soon as we landed. But it was never my way to make things worse if I could help it, so I just went on with my meal—we had come to the dessert now (crepe suzettes too)—and left the Goodsons to pick up the pieces. I had some idea it was something they weren't able to do right away: I didn't imagine so dire a chore had ever befallen them before and perhaps they needed extra time for the ordeal. I did notice that they all of them—parents *and* children—turned their heads away from me and seemed afterwards to concentrate all their attention on a Rotarian and his wife from another Tennessee county who seemed suitably impressed.

Of course I got tickled—mainly just from thinking that a cotton mill (it sounded several steps down from a gin) wasn't all that grand an enterprise and especially after I had heard that the Goodsons originally hailed from Chicago (which, I found out later, was where the cotton mill—or its innards—had come from too) and at first couldn't seem to adjust to the fact that Southerners always took it for granted that everybody was *from* somewhere and usually proud to admit it, something the Goodsons hadn't been used to—like showing their passports every time they crossed a county line.

In short, it all sounded like my mother's always observing that there was nothing like "background" to establish one's place here and now. (It certainly didn't depend on the ownership of cotton mills.) And it really had nothing to do with money or various kinds of "affluence" either but, rather, the way you had been brought up to behave in the world or, as my old nurse, Louella, would have said, "showing your raising," or "what all was behind you." And no, it still didn't have anything to do with money and for that matter, didn't even seem to be showing signs of it any time soon.

The Old Cemetery

Woodville has three cemeteries now: the one called "the Old Cemetery," which was the oldest of the three—down on the street that led ultimately to Long Lake and from there on down to the River, then another one called Oakwood, where a majority of Woodvillians had been buried in the twentieth century (I think there was a sign fixed over the gate that said 1889), and it was built right beside the box factory on the south edge of town, with the Illinois Central Railroad running right by it on the east. But finally the newest of them all was the Barlow County Memorial Gardens about a couple of miles south of town on the Memphis highway; and of course it was laid out in the latest of modern modes, with no mounds over the graves or tombstones at their heads, just flat stones laid on top of them and some sort of metal containers sunk into the ground beside them for flowers.

Of course you could see the influence of the Forest Lawn Cemetery in Glenwood, California, where all sorts of movie stars and other celebrities were buried, writ all over the place. But at least they didn't have Christmas trees on top of all the children's graves as they did out at Forest Lawn when that season rolled around. Still, there were a lot of folks—old ones especially—who didn't care for the idea of being buried out there because the whole thing was built on a hillside. And my seventh-grade arithmetic teacher, Miss Ada Evans, who was a woman of strong convictions and could easily have been the Kaiser of Germany, said she certainly didn't want to be on the drainage side of Miss Carrie Thomas' grave, which that good lady had already arranged for herself, in a "pre-need" plan, right next door, as it were, to Miss Ada.

Miss Ada, of course, never had had much time for her, mainly, I think, because she was suspected of being a Republican (and at that time there were only two "known" Republican families in town). And of course there was no doubt at all of Miss Carrie's being what people called a *big* Baptist and therefore a staunch believer in baptism by immersion—but no baptism at all for children—well, not at least until they reached the age of discretion. (When somebody once asked Miss Carrie how she, who had taught the first grade for forty years, could possibly take such a coldhearted position, she just replied that anybody who had given that much of her life to suffering little children to come unto her would certainly know that the grace of God would have to be twice as strong as it was to ever make much headway there.) And, to sum it all up, if these two stumbling blocks weren't sufficient for the exclusion of non-Baptists, well, you could always fall back on close communion.

Well, that was the layout of the mortuary scene in Woodville. I was of course naturally drawn to Oakwood as the "middle way"—not too decadent, not too modern, like the two others. And of course I knew more people—friends and family—buried there. But of course that didn't keep me from being fascinated with the others. It was mainly the Old Cemetery that especially caught my fancy, and it's somehow difficult to say exactly why. For one thing, it *was* old; and I, who had always been fascinated with the past and all it might convey took a natural interest in it. Just to look at it, when you drove by on your way down to the lake or the river, was almost scary, like a jungle. For one thing, I didn't think the grass and the shrubbery had been cut in fifty years, and on one side it looked positively sinister, with a deep sort of ditch running off from the center of the cemetery down toward a ravine, where there was supposed to be gravel and clay.

At least that's what my schoolmate, John Andrew Ramsay, told me. And we always vowed someday we would make bricks out of it all, though I never knew what for—just a daydream, I suppose. But of course we never did. Anyhow, John Andrew lived right across the street from the entrance to the cemetery and always seemed full of tales about its history—especially anything that smacked of the supernatural. His grandparents lived close by, and I think he had gotten a lot of old tales about the place from them. But I don't think he ever bothered to check them out, as we say. And the Lord knew it was a spooky enough looking place, and so it didn't take much effort on your part to forego exploring the place and just take all the speculation pretty much on faith.

But of course, like all youngsters, we loved a good scare now and then—like the tale about the beautiful young woman who had died suddenly when she was attending a funeral down there some time back during the Civil War. But nobody knew who she was—her name or whether she was from Woodville or elsewhere. And they didn't even know where to bury her. None of her folks showed up to claim her body, so finally the town just had to turn in and take up a collection to bury her right there where she died. And naturally, John Andrew and I were intrigued, especially, when once his grandfather told us some people thought the mysterious corpse was that of an unknown sweetheart who had fallen in love with a Woodville boy when he was fighting in the "massacre" at Fort Pillow.

But neither their families nor friends had ever known anything about it. And the story now went that sometimes the ghost of the lady would rise from her grave in the middle of the night and wander through the cemetery crying and wringing her hands and begging for her sweetheart to come back to her now. It all sounded pretty lurid, but that was what John Andrew's grandfather told us one afternoon when we were sitting out on the porch, all of us drinking Coca-Colas and rocking away in the hot summer time trying to stay cool.

Then there was another story about Mr. Forrest Scott, long after the death of the beautiful lady, and his death wasn't an everyday affair either. He had a grocery store right down on the square. And he was married and doing well in business, but nothing would keep him from going off to the Spanish-American War in 1898. I don't think they had the draft then, and I don't know that he had to *volunteer*. But anyhow away he went down to Puerto Rico—not with Teddy Roosevelt and the Rough Riders but a troop of Tennessee

Volunteers. (Everybody knew our state was nicknamed that because of its generosity with its men in wartime.) And of course the war didn't last but a few months, but somewhere along the line Mr. Scott took a strong liking to bananas (which he had never eaten before) and vowed he was going to start stocking them in his store back in Woodville. Which he did when he came home from the war.

But disaster overtook him one day when he was opening a big carton of the exotic fruit and out came an enormous tarantula and gave him a terrible bite which ultimately proved to be fatal. And it all sounded like a melodrama of "tragedy in the tropics" or something of the sort. So there was a big funeral in the Presbyterian Church and everybody felt very sorry for his wife (who was still a young woman) in her widowhood and of course the children too. Naturally, they buried him in the Old Cemetery, in his family's lot; but every time I walked past it, I wondered if he had had a jinx on him or something, like the beautiful woman who died there. I do know that when his wife died many years later—when John Andrew and I were in high school—they buried her with some of her own folks down at Elmwood Cemetery in Memphis. And I always thought that strange, like maybe they couldn't forgive Mr. Scott for getting bitten by the tarantula and leaving her all alone in the world. But they were some of the Yerger family from down in the Mississippi Delta and, I think, always considered very peculiar.

Well, the Old Cemetery wasn't just a hotbed of the weird and strange, even if some of the oldest families were buried there. O, there are a few more tales I could tell—for example, a brother and a sister who didn't die until well into the 1930s and were then buried side by side. I'm not sure but what they were the last people to be buried there. And I always heard that they considered themselves very much among the elite and "just broken out with aristocracy," as my mother would say.

The family lived right up the street from the Old Cemetery too in what was always mistakenly called an "old colonial home," complete with columns and lots of boxwood. So I suppose they considered no other resting place good enough for them. For all I know, maybe that's why they neither one ever married: again, nobody was good enough. I really had thought they would go to their rest down at Oakwood, but maybe it wasn't ancient enough either. It did look thoroughly funereal, though: pines and cedars all around, even the dark but shiny magnolia leaves. I had heard that old Col. Bryan, who had been in Congress after the War, left the town this tract in his will, but specified that there shouldn't be any pine trees there: they looked too gloomy. But somehow his stipulation was overridden, and they flourished. Only the magnolias bloomed, of course; but in the spring there were dogwoods and redbuds aplenty and they made the place positively brilliant. And somehow they looked more than natural, I thought, not as though they had all come out of mourning.

One thing about Easter I never had liked—the rampant jungle of Easter lilies all over the place no matter where you went, which one of my aunts said always depressed her because they just ran down your throat until you thought you were going to suffocate. In any case, they certainly didn't suggest any kind of resurrection or anything else to do with hope or joy but something dark, gloomy, and well on the way to death. Garden flowers would have been much more appropriate, she said: they stood for spring, the countryside, all that was new and yet natural. Yes, Oakwood was surely better. But then, on down the road, the hillside "memorial gardens" were, let's face it, artificial and tacky as all get out—trying to pretend that death was anywhere else but there. And who did they think they were fooling?

Finally, heading west toward the river, there was the Old Cemetery again—full of the past, full of history, and perhaps full of both the present and the future too. And the dead need not speak: their names and other statistics mostly spoke for themselves—even the mysteries and maybe some strange doings along the way. They needed no footnotes on their behalf, you might say.

One thing, though, I always liked to call attention to after I was grown—a monument erected there in memory of Joseph S. Williams, the author of a book, *Old Times in West Tennessee,* published in 1873—now in print once more through the efforts of one of the local women's book clubs—a kind of history and memoir of our part of the state—personal and yet discreet, telling no tales but thoroughly informed about what one needed to know. And, most importantly, perhaps, setting the balance right for us, West Tennesseans that we were: no, we had no Smoky Mountains, no Hermitage, nor anything else very fancy, whether natural or man-made. But we did have our share of history—nearly all Southern too and not just hanging on by a thread. And yes, what the old folks always said was just about true: it *was* pretty much Three States in One.

Williams's body lay right there just about in the center of things, with what I later learned was a dignified obelisk in the center of his burial plot, circled in by a fence of black chains—thoroughly proud and imposing. I remember that I had known nothing about him until I was, I suppose, in high school; but now I was conscious of what it meant to honor the past as an enrichment of one's own life in the present and likewise as something altogether coherent with the future. For many years, in my own childhood, I knew the Old Cemetery had received little help with maintenance, whether from the town or from private sources. But now I was sure that both the town and its citizens were showing more and more pride in what they really had: more awareness of where they had come from, where they were now and, with luck, where they might be tomorrow. And further, I learned, to my delight, that the husband of one of the club women was now keeping it all regularly swept and garnished every couple of weeks, with the same mower he always used in his own field.

The Devil, Lightning, and Policemen

It's a funny thing, you know, but people are all afraid of different things. Now as for me, I'm mortally afraid of snakes—no matter whether poisonous or not. (I think it has something to do with their perpetual violation of the laws of gravity and traction). And I remember some years ago when after a friend of mine and his family had been living in the Orient for some time, they returned home for a visit and while there kindly urged me to come visit them at my earliest convenience. Which courtesy I appreciated very much but told them I couldn't see my way going to a part of the world where a hooded cobra was as like as not going to greet me at the airport. And of course they died laughing and said, why they had hardly ever seen a snake over there unless it was caged in a zoo and brushed me off by observing that I had seen too many Maria Montez movies when I was growing up—you know, the kind where she played a dusky South Pacific maiden who might—or might not—have inherited an ancestral curse, determining whether she all of a sudden started spitting venom in the most malevolent way, usually at whatever human male was close by and shrinking her eyes at him like she was making an appointment for the future as she quickly slithered away from him into the jungle.

But I didn't bat an eye, thank you. I just told them I had indeed seen more such movies than it would do to tell and furthermore had believed every one of them too. And I've heard no more about the matter since then. But everyone to his own means of exit hence, I always say, to that great zoo up in the sky, to honor the appointment we've all got to keep, sometimes at our own initiation, sometimes not. Certainly the modes preferred by some are not those chosen by others. You can count on that and no questions asked. And funnily enough the differences are often based on what kind of sheer terror

you fancy—not necessarily something of comfort and beauty, like
overdoses of exotic poisons, inhaled or swallowed, to say nothing of
a snakebite or a self-devised exit having to do with tying one end of
an ironing cord around your neck and the other to a balcony railing
on the second floor, then jumping into the void, which thus becomes
more of a strangling than a hanging. But anyhow, as Huck Finn
remarks in quite another context, the wages is just the same. And you
can still name your own poison.

Now Miss Essie Franklin, my first Sunday school teacher, who
lived around the corner from us in the big white-columned monstros-
ity (at least that was what Mamma called it), said she didn't mind a
bit saying she had always been afraid of lightning and policemen—
she didn't know why—and wasn't ashamed to admit it. Maybe, she
said, it was the uncertainty of them both: when policemen went after
you, it might as well have been lightning, it was so sudden and unexpected and of course was accompanied by lots of dramatic equipment
like guns and nightsticks and earsplitting whistles too. And you could
well die of pure stage fright in the process.

But she didn't think it had anything to do with Holy Scripture or
divine vengeance, which most people suspected were just too deep
for us to understand anyhow. If the Lord had made up His mind to
get you, He didn't need any of what Hollywood called special effects.
His very presence sensed nearby could simply scare you to death
without any strain. And then of course things were more smoothly
managed now, she said: there wasn't so much thunder and lightning—what people used to call melodrama—and of course there were
much suaver and more knowledgeable policemen patrolling the
streets. And the more she thought about it, the more credible it
became for modern and progressive times: the scariest things often
were the quietest, she observed, just like in one of those Alfred
Hitchcock movies such as *Rebecca*, where you never saw Mrs.
Danvers, the sinister housekeeper, in motion. All of a sudden she was
just *there* breathing down the second wife's neck and scaring her to
death and you too.

I had a second cousin (by marriage) who was not unlike that lady: she always sidled up to you when you were having a good conversation with her husband (who was the one I was really kin to) and, without saying a word, shoved a post card or a Kodak print into your hands that was supposedly taken when somebody in the family connection (hers usually) had been to Pensacola or Branson, Missouri, or some other tacky spa or downgrade resort. And of course you never knew what to make of it but were afraid to ask for fear she might tell you all about it too—time, place, and genealogy to the third and fourth generation. Or on the rare occasions when she approached you from the front, she held the photograph forward like a dentist's assistant coming at you with a familiar instrument of torture left over from the Spanish Inquisition and you had no place to escape to out of the chair,

Sometimes the logic of all such things—the whys and where-fores—didn't make any sense at all. I know I heard all my life how scary my paternal grandmother was: she was the kind that would run and get under the bed during a thunderstorm—taking the children with her of course—and accordingly almost ruining them for life in the process. And in those days, remember, everybody who lived out in the country had a storm house in the yard and then could relax and say, well, he had done his best, and now it was just in the hands of the Almighty. Which might have been all right for some people, but I always thought you might overbid your hand some day, relying so heavily on your credit with the Power and Light.

I had always felt sure He didn't expect to do it *all* for you: you should show *some* initiative, I thought. But then I had decided some years before that one of the classes of people that were most irritating in the here and now were those that were simply too lazy to *breathe* or else thought all you had to do in this world for safety's sake was sit out on the front porch in the swing most of the day and just wait for somebody to drive up and *carry you off*. And it didn't make much difference who or where, for good or for ill.

But then that's just the way it was with folks, Cousin Ora Belle Jessup always said: she was Mama's cousin and everybody always suspected she had a leaning toward Christian Science. Anyhow, that was what was wrong with people, she said: they were all fearfully and wonderfully made, like the Bible said, and you never could really understand the ways of most of them. And she ought to know, she said: she had taught the first grade for nearly fifty years right there in Woodville. And you needn't to tell *her* about Original Sin, she said. In fact, that was what she had always thought was different about Yankees: anybody that didn't believe in that doctrine but instead preferred to think on "higher things," as they called it, such as the perfectibility of man, was bound to be a fool.

So that was the lowdown on lightning and policemen both—or well maybe one more consideration where the elements were concerned. And that was what some highfalutin people always called the ravages of nature, which I suppose meant what just plain down-to-earth folks would call acts of God. And somehow things seemed more spooky when they were like that—stealing up on you, slowly and silently—again, like snakes or Mrs. Danvers. But I thought you somehow got absolved from the kind of sin that led to that sort of punishment. (It all seemed much more genteel and I wondered was that what grown people meant by the grace of God.) And I just decided that you didn't have to walk around all the time with your tail between your legs, and I just couldn't worry about it all any longer.

Anyhow, that was what I supposed Miss Essie Franklin, my Sunday school teacher around the corner, had some notion of when she just decided to put the whole thing down with "Well, I'm just not going to worry about any of it. When I get my hair—which she didn't *say* but everybody *knew* was dyed—down at night and my teeth out, why, I'd scare Hell out of the Devil himself!" And Mama said well, *she* didn't have any trouble believing that, and she certainly did remember when Miss Essie got her new teeth years ago and Daddy had seen her wearing them for the first time downtown on the

Square and she asked him what he thought about them. And he said you might as well go on and tell the truth and shame the Devil because he himself had worn his for almost twenty-five years and had hated every minute of it, finally concluding, "Essie, you may not realize it yet, but you have had your last good meal!" Tactless, but then what else could you have said, under the circumstances, he wanted to know.

And for what it's worth, I'll just add here that Mamma herself was lucky in the hair question: it was naturally curly. So when anybody ventured to ask her *who* gave her that wonderful permanent and *where*, she just smiled sweetly and said God Almighty had given it to her on the day she was born, which was usually the end of the conversation. So anyhow, there *was* something to be said for mysterious deaths—those arranged by what?—God? nature? foul play?—without consulting any of us? At least you didn't have to die then of pure horror. And maybe that was where the Devil came in: it all just slipped up on you without your expecting any of it and then it was just all over before you knew it. Of course this did have the added element of shock and surprise, but then you didn't have to sit around fearing anything forever and ever, Amen. Maybe it was like what they used to call natural supernaturalism. And you just sat around and *waited*. That seemed about as painless as anything unless you just wanted to go on and get it over with. Of course what the Devil's motive was in all this went by the board: presumably, you had done something that provided him with one.

But however you sliced it, there had to be *some* fear, simply because nobody knew what it would be like; and it would be democratic too—a "first" for everybody. And also you had to take into account the better qualities of even the scary things, as in policemen. I suppose there was never any greater fear in my life than the prospect of being *lost in Memphis*. Where could you go, where could you run to, where could you hide? Well, that was all behind me now, but I did know what a policeman looked like and what their reputation for kindness and protection was. My mother had always told me, in such a case, to go to a central point—a big intersection or an important looking public building—and hunt for a policeman, which wouldn't be hard to do since they all wore uniforms, then tell him my name and my parents' names and address, and ask him to get me back to them. And that never seemed scary—implying anything of the supernatural or the criminal—like kidnaping and so on. And then, my mother would just more or less close her story by saying that I would be immediately restored to my parents, and we would all live happily ever after, and that would be the end of it. Even if some part of the scenario involved death itself—whose it didn't seem to matter—as dangerous and threatening as anything in this world could be, it was a perfectly natural part of life, just like birth. And no worries, no tears, no gloom, no doom. Finally, nothing else except the sure and certain hope that His eye was always on the sparrow. And who could ever ask for more than that?

All under One Roof

My Uncle John, who was a Methodist circuit rider, was Daddy's oldest brother. And he didn't even go into the ministry till he was over thirty, I think, and I never did hear why. Did it take him that long to make up his mind, or was there trouble about money or something of the sort? Certainly, the family never had more than they absolutely needed, and more than once I heard some member of the family say they would all have starved to death if it hadn't been for their mother.

Their father was not any kind of workaholic, and if he decided to go fishing in the middle of cotton chopping, he would just up and do it. Whether this had anything to do with his having been a slave-holder back in Virginia and a Confederate veteran who was at Appomattox into the bargain I have no idea, but certainly his children all treated him with great respect, though mindful of all his foibles too. The day he was buried (at the age of 92), Uncle John's daughter, Mary Virginia, told me she saw one of his sons (there were five of them) who was standing by the fireplace just put his head down on the mantelpiece and give way to a flood of tears; and she said she had never been so sorry for anybody in her life.

But anyhow Uncle John came late into the ministry, and I think one of the local patriarchs (as his children would have been the first to tell you) gave him money from time to time to help with his expenses at the seminary. So of course Uncle John didn't marry till late—in his thirties maybe—and thus got a late start not only in his career but also in starting a family. His wife was Aunt Estelle who, the family all said, had been raised with a silver spoon in her mouth, a phrase which always puzzled me greatly, until somebody explained to me it was all by way of saying that her folks at one time had had money and so she was more or less "used to things" that other folks weren't. But in due course I think the money all played out and she was left with Uncle John on her hands. But they put their shoulders to the wheel and managed somehow to make ends meet: Uncle John as a photographer and Aunt Estelle as a teacher of "elocution" on the side.

Of course it was all naturally hard for them, especially after their three children came along; but they never complained, just enjoyed what they had, Uncle John especially, who grew more and more to love his ministry and to receive much love in return from his parishioners. Of course you could take a dim view of some of that. My mother, who was nothing if not down to earth, said she could have done without so much of the reciprocal affection if only Uncle John had worked harder to get a better assignment in the Memphis conference—a church which paid more, for one thing, and wasn't so far out in the tall and uncut. But nothing like that seemed to be on his mind: indeed, I often thought he seemed really oblivious of the world and all it involved. In any case, he certainly wasn't worried about rendering anything unto Caesar: I think he believed the old boy could just take care of himself. Still, sooner or later most of us have to pay the piper; and if we can't do it ourselves, *somebody* has to do it for us. And it was this side of the question that so annoyed my mother, though I believe my father thought the ministry could do no wrong.

Maybe it was just Uncle John's reading of the Sermon on the Mount. I really never believed he took any thought for the morrow: each day would take care of itself, where feeding and clothing were concerned. And looked at one way, Solomon in all his glory wasn't any competition for faith. But yea, verily, most of us here *are* worldly and find it difficult to divorce ourselves altogether from that allegiance.

Perhaps at no time was Uncle John's love for the family and, indeed, for most of the human race more in evidence than at Christmas, when we had not one Christmas dinner but *five*, one at each brother's house; and then we would be, as he always said when returning thanks beforehand, *all under one roof*, with even a reference to the family members who were no longer in this world. I think Uncle John believed that really made no difference anyway: they were still with us and we with them, only looking forward to the time on that Great Day when we would all be reunited. When that would be seemed to be no concern of his either: that was the Lord's business and not ours. No fire and brimstone sermons for us. And I think he never considered the plight of the wicked on that Great and Dreadful Day either—except to grieve for them for what they were missing.

Perhaps that conjecture tells us more about him than almost anything else: he wanted all of us—and not just the family—to remain together. And I well remember his being careful, when he made the inevitable "group pictures" of the family at Christmas time, to take notice of whatever vacant places in the group there might be, whatever the cause, then calling the neighbors to come fill them up! Sentimental, some people might say, even ridiculous, but not to him: he too wanted his house to be full. And one of the finest sermons I ever heard him preach took its text on the five wise and five foolish virgins: sorrow not fear ruled it all, where evil and wickedness were concerned.

Then I can hear him right now performing the Communion service, especially the rendering of what, I believe, is called the Prayer of Humble Access: "We do not presume to come to this, Thy table, O merciful Lord, trusting in our own righteousness, but in Thy manifold and great mercies. We are not worthy so much as to gather up the crumbs under Thy table. But Thou art the same Lord whose property is always to have mercy. . . . "

His emphasis was always on love and reconciliation—and finally celebration—and of course the group, all to be seated together at the everlasting banquet. And that was just like him: he loved parties, dinners, get-togethers of any kind. And more than once he pointed out how full of social events the New Testament was, beginning with the wedding feast at Cana. And *everybody* was invited regardless of how he ranked in the universal summing up. All that could keep them out was their own refusal of the invitation. If there was any kind of damnation, that would be it, to wake up and realize that it was only you, yourself who had chosen to be so—to be *left out*, probably the most terrifying words in our language, whatever the occasion.

Let the red-hot evangelicals worry about who had been saved and when and where; it was none of their business and perhaps none of yours either. I'll never forget a sermon I heard preached at Christmas time some years ago by a minister who you might say was literally *on fire* with the Good News. And he pled, even begged the congregation to let the Christ Child come into their hearts, to make their greatest decision of all in this world, because some day that tiny helpless little boy, born in a stable, whom no one took any notice of back then, would in due course be THEIR FINAL JUDGE. Christmas has not always been the happiest holiday for me: I've lost several people whom I loved very much at that season. So now it was all I could do to keep from standing up in the sanctuary and hollering "You son of a bitch!" right then and there. Where was the Good News now, where the Joy, and all the rest? It made a mockery of them all. And if I may be so bold, I sensed more malice, more desire to punish than anything else in his words.

This was all a long time after Uncle John's death, but I have a pretty good idea what he would have thought and said. And it was all summed up in the text of the sermon preached at his own funeral: "Take authority to preach the Gospel."

At the Lake

Most people just called it the Lake, but its real name was Deep Lake. And it was second in size, I believe, to every "natural" lake in the state—but by that naturally the TVA lakes were excluded. The largest of the natural ones was of course Reelfoot—formed in the earthquakes of 1811–1812, when the Mississippi River ran backwards for twenty minutes and filled up the places that had sunk in. So it wasn't very deep, and you could see the cypress knees way out in the middle of it all because the lake itself wasn't deep enough to hide them. It got most of the attention too because of the way it was formed, and it was popular with tourists because of the story of its origin and of course its scenic attractions—the dark forests surrounding it—especially the cypress trees—and the waterfowl which populated its environs in the warm, not to say hot, weather in summer. The state government had been scrupulously trying to keep its rarer flora and fauna from becoming extinct too, its biggest success so far being the bald eagle. And so people were hopeful that it would all be restored to its original status in due course.

But Deep Lake in our county was more of a domestic thing—not so much for sightseeing but entertaining and showing visitors what the county was like. But it had its share of atmosphere too. The name itself, for one: *Deep* Lake, which sounded somehow sinister and dangerous, not an altogether comfortable and safe place to just wander around. And it was more "private" too than Reelfoot because a good deal of it belonged to a club of individuals all of whom had to agree when they wanted to entertain outside guests. And the cypress trees and the other trees that, unlike them, grew on the banks, not in the water, helped to intensify the dark and gloomy scene. And, like I said, it was private, almost secluded really, and made you think of Edgar Allan Poe and "The Fall of the House of Usher," maybe even "The Masque of the Red Death"—for that matter, mysteries of all sorts. Was it all just plain old Gothic? Well, I don't think it was only that. Poe himself told somebody his horrors were not from Germany but from the soul itself, and that always made sense to me, whatever their venue was. For that matter, I didn't know that that sort of thing was so scary: it all seemed very old-fashioned now. What could you get out of chains rattling on the stairs these days, to say nothing of secret panels? If the lake had any kind of spookiness, it was more apt to be like something out of a B-grade movie, with comic overtones as well as dark ones.

But somehow you never felt you were altogether welcome down there, and really there were few places to entertain, the principal one being the general store which was where you turned off from the highway that went down to the Mississippi River and you could sometimes stage a fried-catfish dinner on tables with white and red checkerboard cloths, making it all look something like a great pile of Purina feed. And of course anybody that wanted a drink would, in those days, have to supply himself: our county was bone dry. But that of course was no real handicap, just more of an inconvenience, you might say. The counties both immediately north and south of us were both "wet," so nobody really suffered from the drouth.

The camphouses down on the banks of the lake itself, about half a mile from the store, were all privately owned. And sometimes you heard about wild parties being given there by the owners; but nobody really took that too seriously: it was all just part of the scenery and went with the territory, somewhat like a playground. But the most spectacular such jollification that ever took place was, apparently, the socializing put on in one of the houses which belonged to a prominent couple back in Woodville, which of course was up on the bluff some ten or twelve miles from the lake. And they ended up getting a divorce in one of the most spectacular trials ever staged in our courthouse. People even went and took their lunches so they wouldn't have to get up and go home for dinner (the noontime meal in those days) and thus forfeit their seats.

But I'm sorry to say that this was all before my time: well, I was only a year or two old, I believe. So I missed out on all the excitement of both sides suing and countersuing each other and the testimony that, among other things, had the wife kicking up her heels down on the Gulf Coast and sailing around in a yacht that belonged to some big tycoon from Chicago. Meanwhile her husband took their two little boys and went off somewhere down that way too and, we heard, put up at a "hotel" with which he was familiar whose reputation wasn't any better than it ought to be, just so he could keep on eye on her. Yes, there really seemed to be something for every taste in this particular story.

But I heard enough when I got older to deeply regret what I had missed. Really, all of us in my crowd "felt" the loss. And one of my contemporaries (who grew up to be a distinguished gynecologist) said it was one of the great sorrows of his life that he hadn't asked his mother all about it since she was about the same age as the husband and wife involved and naturally went to the trial every day. Then another of my buddies—this one a girl—said she agreed with him, only she had always assumed her mother, who had been the daughter of a Baptist preacher, would be too closemouthed to tell her anything about it all. And so she was afraid to ask her. But shortly before her mother died, she did get up her courage and asked her if she would mind telling her all the lurid details, though I'm sure she wouldn't have used a word like *that*. But her mother just laughed and said she wouldn't have minded telling her about it at all but the trouble was, she had gotten so old she had mostly forgotten all about it and, to tell the truth, she remembered thinking at the time she had heard it all before and it was all pretty dull, certainly compared to what Hollywood was turning out back then—you know, before the Production Code arrived on the scene. But of course we were all really put out with our friends for delaying so long and thus depriving us of what might have been a knock-down-drag-out melodrama told by a real participant therein.

But this was the kind of thing that mostly caused all the talk about what went on at the lake—nothing really scandalous or horrific, certainly nothing like the "night riders" who struck terror into the hearts of the folks up at Reelfoot Lake in 1908, trying to run what they called the "squatters" off the land they claimed to own themselves. And there were disguises (white sheets?) and lynchings and I don't know what all. But no, race had nothing to do with it. It was just a terrorist venture and no more.

Well, we were spared that, thank the Lord. But there was still enough meanness down in the Mississippi Bottom surrounding Deep Lake to keep the sheriff and other officers busy—drinking, gambling, a few pistol and knife encounters, and general carousing around. And O yes, there was some very informal moonshining, the contraband from which often occupied space in the sheriff's office, which was right next to the county library over in the courthouse in Woodville. But none of it created any special havoc, just a few lines in the weekly paper. Certainly, there was nothing like the substantial hullabaloo in all the West Tennessee papers (both Memphis and otherwise) over the Reelfoot episode. Indeed, one summer after I was grown I happened to be visiting some English friends who lived in a beautiful eighteenth-century house down in Somerset; and during the weekend they decided they wanted to attend some sort of athletic meet (gymkhana, they called it) over in the next county. But I decided to stay at home that afternoon, where I entertained myself looking at the files of English periodicals in their library from the early years of the century. And who would have thought it, but what to my wondering eye should appear but an extensive "write-up" in the *Illustrated London News*, carrying both text and photographs, of the Reelfoot affair! Small world indeed and nothing new under the sun.

So, this was more or less all we had to tell about Deep Lake— nothing hair-raising at all, mostly a quiet place to have a camphouse, usually built on stilts or a sizeable mound of earth, to avoid flood damage. It was mainly a place to go hunting and fishing but with little farming: that was for the farmland surrounding the lake whose timber had been all cut years ago. Indeed, one of my high-school teachers recalled its popularity back in the twenties, I think, when the principal gave the whole school a week's fall holiday so they could all go down to the Lake. (She was an ardent fisherwoman herself, so she wasn't altogether a disinterested advocate in the matter.) And there were some who thought that was really the best time to go down there anyway, when the leaves were turning, the cotton was just about ready for picking as you could see in the fields down the road, and the September sun kept up its Indian summer glare and the October nights were moving on toward the chilly.

But it's very different now. There's electricity from the TVA and of course the telephone too, and city water piped all the way over the bluff from Woodville; and the roads are mostly asphalt, not gravel. Many of the houses are quite "modern" now, still built on some sort of stilts but none like in the old days when many of them were built on logs laid flat on the ground beneath them, thus giving them something to float on when the high water came. And there's even some grandeur involved down there too in a Taraesque Southern mansion built across the lake by a big cotton planter that looks very impressive from the boat dock. Of course the levees over in Arkansas throw most of the flood waters over onto the Tennessee side, which have no such protection. And occasionally the Tennessee Bottom has to be *evacuated*, as it was in 1937—when I first learned that word and also another one which came to prominence about that time at the beginning of World War II—*refugee*.

Every year the route of the Mississippi changes a bit, sometimes eroding into Tennessee, at others retreating toward Arkansas. But by and large everybody knows how to face up to it, how to handle it, and the damage and injuries are mostly minimal. But it more or less stays right there just as in Jerome Kern's song in *Showboat*—not talking, not working, not even traveling—still unchanging both today and tomorrow, but always fixed as it was from its origin, forever rolling toward the destination it had chosen from the very beginning.

The Piazza

They were a mother and a son, I supposed, and were handsome people—he, a priest and she, a stylish matron, both in black. And I reckoned he was, say, about thirty, and she was in her middle fifties. It had been a long day for me, seeing sights on this, my first visit to that miraculous city; and I was whiling away the late afternoon by looking at the various people occupying the cafe tables in the square and of course making up stories about them—why they were there, and where they had come from, to sit there in that crepuscular hour in the Piazza San Marco in Venice, seeming to be at loose ends, perhaps wondering where they were going to next.

And I thought of the people who sat in pickup trucks in the hot summer twilight around the square in my hometown back in Tennessee and really didn't see much difference in either. Both groups weren't really *doing* anything; they were just sitting there *looking*, perhaps *waiting*—for what, you might ask. Well, in a time and place like that, it would be whatever happened, whatever came along first. Then what did all those spectators, this audience *think* about the panorama, the procession? Well, nobody could know that either except for what might be its inherent drama and one could only guess at that. But again, I thought of my hometown and O, yes, it was a small world. You didn't have to travel very far or very long to discover that.

Soon now it would be time to get ready for dinner, but for this brief interlude now it was restful, the cafe tables outside their respective buildings, some of them elegant or even enchanting, the small orchestras outside to help one recollect or even solidify the thoughts and happenings of the day and of course begin to think and plan for the next time. First, Florence probably and then maybe on to Rome, and we would be getting most of the Renaissance in one fell swoop. And no, you couldn't take it all in then, just try to absorb something of the atmosphere, pick out what you relished most, and of course start planning for your next trip, when you would have had your introduction and now, as a veteran, wanted to broaden it, deepen it. And of course you couldn't just *inhale* it in such a short visit, only look and listen, getting some idea of what the scene was like, whence it acquired its multifarious magic, hastily looking in one way to absorb the scene—first of all, naturally the other tourists like ourselves—the people in the Piazza, then quickly turning around and looking at the lagoon and if possible looking on out as far as the Lido and the Adriatic itself.

And all the while the aimless wandering of tourists and the people who were their leaders on their respective pilgrimages, the sound of the motorboats—which served as the city buses—arriving beside the Doge's Palace to discharge one group, then collect more for the homeward journey and once more fading away into the distance. All of it some sort of drama enacted endlessly every day and yet somehow never losing its magic, especially for whoever was paying his first visit there.

And then I happened to turn around to look at the facade of St. Mark's once more—Byzantine, maybe Gothic, as well as whatever was strictly its own—right in the center of this enchanted city, ridiculous, even preposterous in some ways, sitting out there in the lagoon, all by itself, with the Grand Canal opening into it too and thus disposing of the city's wastes, meanwhile caring nought for what you as visitors might think of it all.

And then suddenly I saw what I had assumed earlier was the same mother-and-son couple; and as far as I could tell, they had hardly changed their view of their surroundings and perhaps had no more to say to each other than they had had when I first spotted them. And I wondered even more now what they were all about—a son whose priestly vows were now final and a mother who was only beginning to grasp the significance of it all—and perhaps wonder was it all worth it. No, he would never marry now nor would she have any grandchildren either. But then were they really going to miss the daughter-in-law wife and perhaps another generation too? Who could tell, for that matter? But their facial expressions, I thought, revealed a great deal.

He sat there looking far off, out toward the sea—perhaps wondering, thinking, even meditating; she, however, had turned her back on that, her eyes examining somewhat aimlessly the faces of all those wanderers in the square. And I wondered what she was seeing there—or what she was thinking. Were they in any way resentful of what each had given up for the other or, for that matter, something far more important than either? And how long had this new status been their world? Had they had time to adjust to it all? Had they tried but perhaps found it less than prepossessing? And did the young man, particularly, have any regrets?

Dark-complexioned but not swarthy, he was a handsome young fellow, just as what I had assumed was his mother, in her quietude and tranquillity, seemed somehow remote and serene from the world which enveloped us all. Elegant, stylish, they could not have been undervalued anywhere. But now I suddenly realized that they were speaking excellent English when, all along, I had supposed them to be of Latin descent. But again, you couldn't have classified that as a mystery of any sort. Certainly, Henry James would never have assumed it so. And yes, all of us, according to the Bible, were fearfully and wonderfully made. And no, it didn't have to make any *sense* either. For that matter, where was the woman's husband, the young man's father? Again, who knew, even perhaps cared? And had they now exhausted all they had to say to each other until their next meeting? And when would that be anyhow? No, it wasn't really a mystery, perhaps just a puzzle, maybe even something of a tease, one simply given us (by whom and for what?) to increase our wonderment at our own lives and, finally, the marvel of our own world.

Connections

Our town, Woodville, was situated right on the main line of of the Illinois Central Railroad—usually referred to, in its advertisements, as the "Main Line of Mid-America." Roughly parallel to the Mississippi River, which lay twenty miles to the west, it was part and parcel of the Mississippi River Valley and its culture and was often referred to, if not as the "I.C.," simply "the Railroad," just as the Mississippi itself was known as "the River" and "the Late Unpleasantness" of the preceding century as "the War." And Woodville itself was quite dramatically situated about halfway between its termini of Chicago to the north and New Orleans to the south; and quite often the daytime streamliners, the "City of New Orleans," one headed north, the other south would pass each other in mid-afternoon right there—the whole thing enhanced by the double-tracks and automatic block signals in use back then, implying that the whole thing was a class act.

The north- and southbound versions of the overnight crack train (all-Pullman and extra-fare too)—the "Panama Limited" as it was called—often did likewise, though hardly anybody was ever there to see them meet at that late hour since neither they nor the "City of New Orleans" actually stopped there. (Woodville was too small for that and somehow it didn't seem to matter anyhow: the Panama's high speed and the resulting commotion only enhanced the drama.) But sometimes you would wake up in your own bed around midnight and hear the two "Panamas" blow for Woodville and for each other, so you knew all was well and under control and on time.

Perhaps the Illinois Central was not without a sense of history too, as well as geography. Its Central Station in Chicago—right off the Loop on one side and Lake Michigan on the other—had been built for the World's Columbian Exposition of 1892–1893, the fair which so excited Henry Adams; and indeed the "Panama" itself was supposedly named to celebrate the immense Central American banana trade (after all, New Orleans was the second port in the nation) and perhaps the Canal itself though that didn't actually materialize until a couple of decades later, duly celebrated in 1915 by the Panama-Pacific International Exposition in San Francisco—just in time for World War I. Yes, the I.C. had a sense of them both—past and present, history and geography too.

I was even told once that the reason so many students from the South continued their graduate work at the University of Chicago rather than at the older Eastern schools was its geographic inevitability and furthermore the same logistics had had a hand in persuading other Southerners to head for Minnesota and the Mayo Clinic, not Johns Hopkins, if they were seriously ill. And along the way there was plenty of scenery, not just something picturesque to be admired but something to be viewed with respect—Lake Michigan, the Ohio junction with the Mississippi at Cairo, the smooth and seemingly endless prairies of the Midwest with their "corn knee-high by the Fourth of July"—marvels all of them, not just something else to be conquered. Nature, weather, all the "givens" were after all the ones calling the shots here; and you would do well to adapt yourself to the realities, not the reverse. And perhaps that was part of the ultimate fascination for me: you played by their rules, not your own.

And yet the ingenuity of man was not wanting either. After all, it was the steel rails, designed and fabricated by man himself, which here carried the great forces where he willed, in our case all the way to Chicago and the Lakes in the north, then all the way southward to New Orleans and the Gulf, even branches leading to both Louisville and St. Louis. And extremes of climate, terrain, time, and place were not wanting (blizzards in the north, hurricanes in the south) quite fitting for a land so diversified, so much its own master. And perhaps that was the real fascination of the trains for me and many others—not only an exultation in their achievements in transportation but a kind of triumph, celebration they imposed on the land—time and place themselves—but, mind you, always with due respect. (These were people, remember, who never forgot that the earth was the Lord's and the fullness thereof.) Even men—and American men at that—knew who was the boss in all such matters. And the be-all and end-all, the rationale of the whole business itself was finally *making connections*, bringing people and their wares together at their common destination. I had somehow sensed this from my earliest childhood—all of it on time, nothing left to chance, all predictable. . . . And the station agent could always tell you where the train was *right that minute*, with no stone left unturned, and no surprises.

The bottom line, you might say, was there for all to see, certainly in the great "union" stations of our big cities—in the central dramatic feature embodied in the ubiquitous *clock* which usually towered over the building itself, showing the whole world exactly what you could expect and of course thereby commanding the respect of all. And in short, it was all something you could *count on*, unlike what you might feel about buses or airplanes or other modes of movement. On occasion it might seem they kept their appointments with whim or caprice, even irresponsibility. And often it didn't seem to matter: with the motor vehicle it may have been informality that carried all before it, with the airplane it was speed—and much of it highly informal too! Furthermore, you were always more or less helpless in their hands. Indeed, an old friend of mine once referred to the mode of the train as *travel*, while that of all the others was *transit*. And furthermore, she said she didn't ever again want to ride *anything* where she couldn't tell them to stop and let her off if necessary!

But again, the emphasis was all on what you could expect, what you could more or less set your watch by. I remember my father telling me that all the railroads in the country—their time, their schedules—were regulated by a central control system based in Washington. And whatever time was laid down there was what the whole country followed, making allowance of course for different time zones. The key to the whole system came when the noon hour was struck from there every day of the week—what went out to every railroad station in the country in a signal which sounded like the mild "tick" of a telegraph instrument—mild in sound but gigantic in significance. And there was no guess work about any of it. *Time* then was the essence of the whole concept: that was its master and its attraction, towering above all in the dominant station clock, which sometimes flaunted a Mercury-like figure from its pinnacle, to show who and what was in command—something like fortune or fate, something you couldn't argue with. Indeed, you almost bowed your head accordingly. And it all originated in Washington, just as the rails, the tracks themselves began and ended, for the I.C., in Chicago and New Orleans. And it was all *connected.* And though my father always refused to change his watch whenever he had to leave the Central Standard Time zone, even he had to submit to this fundamental principle.

Well, this of course was only part of its hold, part of the drama which held you fast, your attention never faltering. Because embodied in the whole concept was something almost mystical, almost like magic. *Look*—there was all that speed, all that power and yet all of it ultimately controlled by ribbons of steel only four feet, eight and half inches apart, a steel highway, if you will, all dependent for direction on a surface no wider than a piece of chalk. But this tiny surface, this delicate control had the last word, and its word was law, wherever it was headed. And so the gigantic force, the pride of time and place which was this monstrous creature was directed and controlled by something like a microcosm, a never-failing device you could, again, count on. Something of course which had to obey you, provided you played by the rules of the game yourself—all balance, all harmony you might say. And nobody failed to believe in it, to accept its dignity and pride. People across the country would set their watches by the most prestigious trains, never doubting their reliability except in the most extraordinary circumstances—floods, blizzards, tornados, all agents of the unpredictable—all that trains were not.

And when I speak of drama here, I mean just what I say. To hear the whistle of a steam locomotive several miles away, especially at night, to *know* exactly when you could expect it at your station with bells ringing and steam pouring forth like a volcano, with dignity and force, was not to be ignored—right on time, nearly always true to the where and when—something like an old friend: these were the greatest of gifts, reassurances. And then the arrivals by night, which my father always said made everything feel spooky—the wind whistling around the station's eaves, as it sat there in the midst of almost total darkness, then the headlight which you could glimpse down the track, sometimes even around a corner, not seeming to slow down at all except just as it pulled up to the station waiting room, Because it knew you would wait for it, and you knew it was always in control. And thereby you knew what an *entrance* was like, like something on the stage or screen: bold and peremptory, it was not something you could ignore. And the very idea of *missing* it was unimaginable if not intolerable.

✳ ✳ ✳

Trains had a glamor then, no doubt about it. But even more than glamor there was a force, a necessity which commanded all the rest. Because if they often led to romantic journeys and exciting things you couldn't say nay to, they often foreshadowed things that were portents of disturbance, disasters which you ignored at your peril, to say the least. After all, it was on trains that dead bodies were shipped home from big city hospitals, transports which brought back disasters from the battlefield and the ominous news brought by newspapers and telegrams—none of it pleasant. And this was its business side— no excursions, no gaieties here. And again, it was not anything you could ever argue with. Once when my mother's father, who had been Woodville's Marshal for years untold—you could always spot him on his big gray stallion, they said, in a procession, a parade or whatever the occasion—was down at the station, waiting for the arrival of a desperately sick lady from a tuberculosis sanitarium, he was right there to help remove her stretcher from the baggage car where they always carried the dying and the dead in those days. And I never forgot what she was supposed to have said to him when she looked up and saw him there: "Mr. Wood, I've come home to die." And that was all that was necessary, though it had all the overtones of *Camille*. I couldn't imagine buses or airplanes arriving in such circumstances: with them there was no ceremony.

Well, they're more or less all gone now—the big steam locomotives, with their glitter, their power. And I remember when the streamlined, diesel-equipped "Panama" first charged through the deep cut right in the middle of town under what was called the "overhead bridge," just after World War II began. And you could hear its big flat whistle, sounding just like what it was—a machine, and you could see its big electric headlight going back and forth making a monstrous figure "8", all in the interest of safety and security. But it was all too mechanical, all too artificial for my taste—and I gather, the taste of many others. There was no particular drama, no vibrant life, to set it all wild and free. Instead, there was only the more or less calmly efficient and predictable, just as you might have expected—not the "on time" shibboleth always demanded of the bold chargers in the old days. Now there were no exceptions, no variety to heighten one's excitement, his participation in the whole scene, no drama either. Instead, just the inevitable predictability, with no surprises and no excitement.

* * *

Long after I had left Woodville and gone off to school, every time I came home for a visit I would sooner or later go down to the depot, to see what was going on. Of course the best time was mid-afternoon, when I could see the "City of New Orleans" groaning its way round the bend at the end of the cut, even if I was lucky, see the two "Cities" meet right in front of the station and know that their passengers were exactly halfway through their respective journeys, wondering about them, what they thought of the journeys' ends they were approaching, what they hoped or feared as the result, wishing too that I might be on there with them—the excitement, the mystery it might hold for me.

On the other hand, I could recall some actual memories about the "Panama" because part of my schooling had taken place in Chicago and sometimes I came home by that route, leaving there about 5:00 in the afternoon, arriving up the road from Woodville around midnight at a larger, more important station. And there were lots of memories to call up after that: a seat in the observation car since there were no "day coaches" available, a "club car," where I could sit reading, say, one of Conrad's or Hardy's novels, at nearly 100 miles an hour, with a martini in my hand, oblivious to all except the soft, swift swaying of the car as we sped down the Illinois prairie. And then duly taking myself back to the diner—two units, one for dining, the other for cooking—for one of the I.C.'s fine dinners, especially when seafood reigned supreme. And naturally it would often do so since their trains went in and out of New Orleans every day. Then a liqueur to finish off with before returning to the observation car, where the lights were now dimmed and you could sit watching the world outside lit up—for Christmas if it was that time of year or hot summer time which you could only *feel*. And since you were in the last car, it often felt as though you were at the very tail of some lightning-like animal or even a comet, which was giving you a larruping-fast ride for all it and you were worth.

Then as the evening waned and passengers sitting beside you might begin to nod, your own spirits would rise expectantly at the thought of home and family which now drew nearer every minute. First there would be the Ohio to cross at Cairo, safely of course at only twenty miles an hour, I was told, then some miles of running right beside the moonlit Mississippi as it slowly but steadily moved south on its way to Memphis and the Delta. Then ultimately to "The Big Easy," as New Orleans was sometimes called, and finally into the Gulf itself and the wild freedom lying ahead. Soon now there would be the slowing down and grinding of brakes and you would get your things together and make your way to the door leading back into the

Pullmans and other cars, all ready now for the dramatic arrival just ahead, no matter how often you had done it before.

And finally, in what might have been one of my last such home-comings, I was suddenly presented with something like a splendid surprise, perhaps as a sort of benediction to all these years of adventure: the train made an extra stop. It was Christmas and an even larger crowd than usual seemed on board—more cars, more people. So the train stopped first where it usually did—its length about halfway beyond the station. But that apparently didn't seem adequate enough to "discharge" so many passengers, so the "Panama" pulled up until the observation car was halted right in front of the station. And now looking around, I saw that there was nobody else waiting to get off there but me; so I raised my questioning eyes to the conductor, whom I thought I recognized from previous journeys. And he bowed and smiled as if by way of saying yes, go ahead. Could anything in my life, my career ever have been more exciting? Was it all some kind of reward for my lifelong fidelity to this mode of transportation and my old friend, the I.C.? Perhaps even then I might have had some sort of idea that this might be one of the last of my train journeys, so dwindling did the trains seem to be in numbers and frequency as the years fled on.

Well, so be it. Perhaps, in addition to my smiles at seeing my parents again, there were a few tears also. But again you gave thanks for what you had been given, been allowed as sure and certain, what finally you could count on. And that ultimately was all that mattered, with trains or anything else.

Let There Be Light

That summer when I was twelve was the first one after Pearl Harbor, when on the national scene they were preparing frantically to throw the might of the whole country into war but locally were completing the new Methodist Church out at Maple Grove, the community where my father and all his brothers had grown up. And, in addition, almost daily they were expecting the advent of the new miracle of electricity, made possible on the rural scene by the Tennessee Valley Authority. Actually they had started on the church the previous fall because they wanted to have it ready by summer time, when they always had their revival; and as a matter of fact had even had it dedicated by the bishop right after Thanksgiving. (It was the first time I had ever seen a bishop, methodist or otherwise; and frankly, I thought it somewhat disappointing: he didn't wear anything like a robe or a gown, just a plain business suit and certainly no pointed hat—which I later learned was called a mitre—at all.) But the summer was when they had their biggest crowds, especially after laying-by time, when the crops had been worked all that was necessary and there was nothing for you to do except wait for them to mature. And the church naturally wanted to be able to have the grand opening to coincide with the arrival of the new light. And if that sounds like a bad, even irreverent pun, perhaps there's more truth in it than first appears.

The TVA was naturally a big thing for us and, in fact, as some people put it, including my father, would probably take us from one century to another overnight. Of course, as you could expect, there were folks out there and in other parts of the country too who disapproved of the whole thing: it would probably increase taxes, they said, and undermine private enterprise and extend the power of the federal government and such like. But Daddy said they had never stopped to think about the number of people whose lives were shortened because the drudgery of the old days, which he always ironically referred to as the "bad old days," had positively worked them to death. And why should they not have "modern conveniences" anyhow, just like everybody else? After all they paid taxes too or if not that enabled other people to pay theirs.

And I would certainly go along with Daddy's position for no other reason than the fact that I got tired of going to the outhouse in all weathers and trying to read by lamplight when we went out to my Uncle Jim's, whose house was just down the road from the church. One time, I remember, when I went outside for my bodily necessities, I had even gotten jumped by the old rooster who regarded the whole back yard as his domain and—who knows?—if I hadn't had on my leather or "bomber's" jacket, as it was often called then, might have been severely scratched or otherwise injured. But when it came down to convenience and safety, I was always on the side of modern times, for all the fact that my father's family always spoke up for the quality of life, the affection and of course the cuisine which had pervaded their house down the road from my uncle's—"The Home Place," as they called it—when their parents were alive. (But, with her customary realism, my mother said they were just all getting old, and that was the whole trouble, pure and simple.) And, truly, as in all other things, when it came right down to it, as a family, they were always on the side of reason and good sense—good sensible Methodists with nothing fanatical about them. And they well understood the advantages of the modern age and its conveniences and anything else that seemed to cut down on needless effort. But no, they didn't regard themselves as servants of the machine, nor did they think you could live by bread alone.

Moonlight nights and my aunt's roses (particularly the flesh-pink Dr. Van Vleet and the paper-white Silver Moon) growing on the barnyard fence were romantic to them in the lamplight, as was my father's favorite love song, "Moonlight and Roses." And to this day I can still hear the rise and fall of their voices as we sat in the front yard with only the lamplight spilling outwards from the house to give us what illumination we needed, and the only other sounds the swing's back and forth rhythm softly squeaking in the near-dark. Sometimes there would be a prime watermelon cutting from the wonderful produce of my uncle's summer crop, with the accompanying cries of pleasure and enjoyment. And it was all tranquil and domestic and secure. And the war and human suffering, even death itself seemed very far away.

For a while my uncle had had carbide lamps in the house, but they apparently made too much noise (a sort of hissing) and perhaps even the threat of fire for people to be completely at ease with them. So in due course I think he gave them to the church, to tide them over till the electricity had arrived and was installed up there, while we ourselves waited: I believe my uncle thought their need was greater than his. But even then I somehow didn't quite believe in what miracle lay ahead, I had been used to the lamplight so long.

And to tell the truth, there was something moving about things like music in the twilight, and always when it was church hymns from up the road (when we ourselves weren't able to attend), the grace and joy they brought to whoever heard them from a distance: "When the Lord said whosoever / He included me," then "Walk in the light, beautiful light / Shine all around us by day and by night," and "He's the Lily of the Valley / The Bright and Morning Star," even on to "Brighten the corner where you are" and all else that suggested the eternal light shining in darkness, the morning star, and the Word made flesh, forever full of grace and truth.

Really, who would want to change that for the electric, the automatic, and the quiet? but this family knew better, knew it had to come if we were to dwell in anything like future peace and plenty, not forswearing the good life they had always known but embracing ways and means that would make their world adaptable to the new ways and a life of less drudgery and greater comfort. And accordingly, they made themselves ready for the dawn, for this new world.

And so it came to pass, around the first of August, appropriately enough just in time for the "big meeting," not like a thief in the night, but slowly and surely as the sun was sinking and the twilight growing, and we more or less held our breath at the wonder of it all, from the church up the road, its lights all lit and shining, to where we sat there in my uncle's yard and waited for the church to blossom into a city set on a hill and become finally a beacon to us and the whole creation. And somehow, it did just that—giving light to all within the house and all of us who sat outside in expectation and wonder. Surely, none of us then could ever forget this, our first experience of the new world, all those years ago, or even now as a few of us are still left to stand on the verge of yet another dawn, a new millennium.

The Last Day, an Epilogue

The day had finally arrived, the one I had learned early to expect, even fear from my earliest recollections all those years ago. I would say almost feared from the beginning—the time when I would become more than ever a traveler, with no parents, no brothers and sisters—when I would have to make my own way as best I could. I wasn't a babe in arms of course but nearly fifty, and I had been born late (my parents were both in their forties at the time) and I knew I would have to fend for myself from this on out.

Of course I had known early on that I would probably lose my parents before my schoolmates lost theirs. And I had only a few cousins, about whom I was uncertain as to whether they liked me or just put up with me, so far up the ladder of years they were ahead of me. But for a good many years of course my life underwent few changes—certainly not cataclysmic ones: truly then it was just my mother and father and me.

But when I was in my teens, my mother had great difficulty with her menopause—depression, anxiety, and all the rest, had to stay in a hospital in Memphis for a month or six weeks and if truth were told, perhaps never got over what most people then called the change of life or, euphemistically, a nervous breakdown. One of the elderly cousins on my mother's side of the house even suggested to me that her own mother, my grandmother, had had something like this illness; and at the least was often thought to be "peculiar," that catch-all in Southern speech which often covered a multitude of sins, whether of the mind or body. But of course very little was known about treating such things back then. (Were they genetic or was the victim just often dismissed as bad-tempered and spoiled rotten?) But gradually my mother came back to "normal" though for the rest of her life she was inclined to come down with occasional "setbacks" which came on suddenly for no apparent reason.

My father was different of course: he had a real temper and it came and went quite often. But you would never have said he had any kind of mental problems. Loving us both so much, he seemed never to give a thought to that sort of thing, sometimes even seemed to be really put out with my mother and sometimes even me for being so "sensitive" and quick to falter along the way. And so I wondered what would happen to me in the fullness of time, after they were gone and I had nobody more or less to belong to or, as Carson McCullers might have put it, nobody to be *included* by. But I tried my best always to just live each day by itself, maybe even like the Good Book says, taking no thought for the morrow—but of course sometimes more easily said than done.

Finally when I had gotten out of college, even held a graduate degree, I knew the time—or rather, the day—had come when I would have to make all my arrangements for myself. But again, easier said than done. By then I had more or less come to accept the fact that I would probably never have a family all my own—no wife, no children. But some people were never satisfied with just a *statement* about such things, they wanted to know the whys and wherefores. So I finally worked out what I considered to be a tactful if noncommittal answer: "Well," I would say, "those matters either arrange themselves or not at all." And that would settle the matter, at least for my inquisitors. (One of my aunts, who came from an extremely close-mouthed family, observed that it might not be a bad thing just to ask my cross-examiner why he wanted to know in the first place. But I think I was still too shy to go that route.)

Had my parents somehow done me a disservice along the way, treating me like a child in some ways, but unable to fathom the work I had been doing, and the special universe one might say I had been living in—first, in school, then my job itself. They both should have known better. And I wondered whether I should have fought against this more than I did. A long time ago I had decided that the people who do get eaten up in this world always, whether they realize it or not, have decided to go along with whatever somebody else plans for them. I'm not sure exactly why: maybe they don't want to hurt the aggressor's "feelings" or their spirit has been so much weakened they don't have any energy left. But it's not an admirable situation for either party.

In any case, it was not my mother who died first but my father, one morning when we were having breakfast during my visit home for the Easter weekend. I had gotten up to pour myself some more coffee when there was this absolutely horrific crash and there he lay beside his chair, dead as a stone, with no last words or any other dramatic moments. And after that my mother really began to go downhill rapidly but still survived him by ten years. And I learned there and then that no matter when death came, you were never ready for it and furthermore, there was no really "good" way to die. My father couldn't have died more quickly, and yet I knew that had been the way he always said he "wanted to go." But later during my mother's long, long illness it seemed as though she could never die— or at least not until she was ready. And I think some of the family were even of the opinion that they were going to have to knock her in the head on Judgment Day. Strangely enough, though, she retained her sense of humor all the way. When she complained to me once about the noise and foul language so many of the patients were responsible for in the hospital where she lived her last years, I responded by saying, "Well, come now. You haven't heard any words you didn't already know, have you?" And just like her old self, she responded with "Well, no, but some of the combinations have been unusual."

So there it was: I was all alone now, just as I had expected to be. But no, I wasn't lonely. Surely, I wanted to be around other people, to see my childhood friends, to take part in life and all that went with it. But no, I never wanted to live *with* anybody or anything; it was too late for that, I was sure. And also I didn't realize it at first, though our town and county, indeed the whole state were important to me. I knew by now that I didn't really want to *belong* to any of them either. And so that's the way it was: I duly became a teacher, yes, a real live professor at the state university and could more or less make my own way wherever I wanted to go—but, as I've said, not ever lonely. I somehow didn't ever feel the need for that. I seemed to get my own joys from my teaching, trying to communicate with students across what often seemed like astronomical distances. But I derived some wry humor from the reflection that that was what every teacher worth his salt was trying to do, even poor Christa McAuliffe of the Challenger disaster who was literally going to try teaching her own students "back home" a lesson from "outer space"—which is more or less the penalty exacted from every teacher in the business. And it's the duty of us all—to try again and again to bridge the distance between the desk and the audience; and in some ways our task is no more—and no less—than that. So I simply went on ahead with my life, which was a good one, living it just as I wanted to, and not really sad for anything else. By this time both my parents were gone, even the aunts and uncles going fast now too: all of them now in their late sixties and beyond and apparently never minding the future.

But I think I did because somehow I felt I hadn't lived my whole life—always living from the inside out, not by any means experiencing the whole show. And I would think of Henry James's Strether in *The Ambassadors*, who urged the American to "live your life" and not miss out on anything, you might say: the world was too rich, too wonderful for that.

Now of course I had "no fixed address" as it often says of the suspects in English detective stories; I was in the sere and yellow leaf right that minute. (That was one thing in the world which you never had to work at.) And as one pair of aunts and uncles (there were five of them, counting my father and mother) would die off, I would realize that I would have to change my dwelling when I came home during my infrequent visits. And with friends likewise. I had sold our house long ago; indeed sometimes I didn't really feel that I had a home anywhere, maybe never had had one. As I said, I was always the stranger, the outsider with not even a place to lay my head, which sounded biblical and melodramatic at the least. But on the other hand, I wasn't surprised by any of the consequences: that was my life just the way I had seen it coming from the deep past itself. And I seemed to know all along it would be mine and, for that matter, sooner or later everybody else's too. And the shadows and ultimately the darkness would engulf us all. Sometimes gradually, sometimes not, as in the case of my parents. But still there was *something* to miss, the same old friends, the sights and sounds of my hometown, the things, the people, both old and young, who were still themselves yet ever changing too. That was the very substance of life.

But I was not unhappy to live like that, I think: they were all still *my* people and yes, I *still* belonged there. But now it was headed for a conclusion, even if nothing more than "lights out." And now it was possible that the end was in sight: the last of the aunts and uncles had died. And I knew now this was "the last day" I had been expecting for so many years—not in fear so much as in impatience. What was it going to be like for me—alone now, presumably from this on out, and not *with* anybody? I didn't owe anybody anything either, though I had always been trained to pay my way, in both shadow and substance, whatever I did, wherever I went. Yes, I was free all right; but then up to a point anybody could be free. Was that like a cautionary piece of advice, to be careful because you might get what you prayed for? Who could say, who really knew? You might simply have to put the bit between your teeth, in your own mouth, looking forward and not backward. And be beholden to no man. There were going to be no instant solutions in the matter; I knew that much. But it was going to be a time of trial for me, there was no doubt. I could see myself toiling in the field again and again; but, for what it was worth, waxing stronger every time I went forth.

* * *

So now that's what I was meditating on as I drove forth on that day from the house where in his last days my grandfather had lived and now the aunt and uncle, who were the last of that generation. Their son and his wife would, like it or not, sell it and probably move to Memphis—no more than I would expect now. And if I had been in their shoes, I might have done the same.

But not now: somebody had to be custodian of all those family tales and the characters themselves depicted therein. But not me: I was still the outsider looking in, with perhaps double vision which could see both sides. But for that kind of situation somebody had to remain on the spot, not just wax and wane like the moon. People like me made excellent messengers; but no, they were not living on the stage where it had all taken place. But now I had said my goodbyes to the aunt and uncle's son and his wife and whatever other cousins remained and now as I pulled out of their driveway for what might be the last time, I reflected on the fact that I had always been called a "safe" driver who thought everything through as he drove away, very cautiously but by no means fearful of the whole enterprise that he was embarking on now. So now I looked to the left up the gravel road which led right by the Methodist Church where all my father's family had been baptized and in due course finally buried. And there was the farm where all the family had congregated on festive occasions, where my grandparents had lived when they first married, especially on Christmas and many Sundays throughout the year—where they had all grown up—"the home place," as they all called it. And then farther on down the other way, to the right, where, after crossing the railroad on the rickety old bridge I could pick up the highway down south to Memphis or even northward where in about two or three hours I would be crossing the Ohio River, leaving the South altogether behind. Would I decide to leave my present situation and go try my hand at some other? I had always thought changes were good for most people from time to time. Or would I elect to stay in my own country, my own teaching where I always felt secure and stable? It was obviously going to be a hard decision.

But perhaps such things did you good too—trying yourself against whatever difficulties might come your way, pitting your strength against the adversaries and perhaps strengthening whatever was in you in the act. Whatever the case, I felt I would never look back, dwell in the past. Really, I didn't need to; the memories were right there inside me. But I knew also that I would never let them go—even if I thought I could. They were very much in the baggage I carried with me, and would forever be so, whatever I did, wherever I went.

The Picture Frame and Other Stories
by Robert Drake

ISBN 0-86554-689-4. Warehouse and catalog pick number: MUP/H510.
Copyright ©2000. Mercer University Press, Macon, Georgia 31210-3960.
Text and interior designs, composition, and layout by Edmon L. Rowell, Jr.
Cover and dust jacket designs and layout by Jim Burt.
Camera-ready pages (xiv+176) composed on a Gateway 2000 386/33C
    and on an AOpen BG45-AP5VM via dos WordPerfect 5.1
    and WordPerfect for Windows 5.1/5.2, and printed on a LaserMaster 1000.
Printed and bound by McNaughton & Gunn Inc., Saline, Michigan
    via offset lithography on 50# Writers Natural;
    Smyth sewn and cased into Roxite B cloth with one-hit gold foil,
    with 80# natural endsheets, and with dust jacket printed black plus
    three PMS colors on 80# Litholabel, layflat matte film laminated.
                                                      [April 2000]

                                                      [041900elr]

5/0,

Drake
The picture frame

GAYLORD S